## WHAT SHE NEEDED

She wanted nothing more than to rest her head on his shoulder and to feel him wrap his arms securely around her.

He bent down and very gently pressed his lips to hers.

Immediately, Rose felt a rush of tingles through her body. Warmth followed, welling up in her breast. Without worrying about what he would think of her, or whether or not she was doing the right thing, she allowed herself to just relax and kiss him back.

And she also found that she needed to wrap her arms around his neck and hold on to him—just in order for her knees not to completely give way.

It felt so good, so right to be in Sinjin's arms.

# BOOK YOUR PLACE ON OUR WEBSITE AND MAKE THE READING CONNECTION!

We've created a customized website just for our very special readers, where you can get the inside scoop on everything that's going on with Zebra, Pinnacle and Kensington books.

When you come online, you'll have the exciting opportunity to:

- View covers of upcoming books
- Read sample chapters
- Learn about our future publishing schedule (listed by publication month *and author*)
- Find out when your favorite authors will be visiting a city near you
- Search for and order backlist books from our online catalog
- Check out author bios and background information
- Send e-mail to your favorite authors
- Meet the Kensington staff online
- Join us in weekly chats with authors, readers and other guests
- Get writing guidelines
- AND MUCH MORE!

**Visit our website at
http://www.kensingtonbooks.com**

# DAME FORTUNE

*MEREDITH BOND*

**ZEBRA BOOKS**
Kensington Publishing Corp.
www.kensingtonbooks.com

ZEBRA BOOKS are published by

Kensington Publishing Corp.
850 Third Avenue
New York, NY 10022

All Kensington titles, imprints, and distributed lines are available at special quantity discounts for bulk purchases for sales promotion, premiums, fund-raising, educational, or institutional use.

Special book excerpts or customized printings can also be created to fit specific needs. For details, write or phone the office of the Kensington Special Sales Manager: Attn. Special Sales Department. Kensington Publishing Corp., 850 Third Avenue, New York, NY 10022. Phone: 1-800-221-2647.

Zebra and the Z logo Reg. U.S. Pat. & TM Off.

ISBN 0-8217-7822-6

First Printing: September 2005
10 9 8 7 6 5 4 3 2 1

Printed in the United States of America

*To my father,*
*my greatest cheerleader*

# PROLOGUE

Sated after a delicious morning of lovemaking, Sinjin lifted himself up to rest on one elbow and looked into Georgiana's heavy-lidded eyes. Life could not get any better than this.

"*Nunc scio quid sit amor,*" he said, teasingly because he knew how it bothered her when he quoted the classics.

She scowled at him and then waited for the translation.

"Now I know what love is," he said, running his hand down her naked body, enjoying the familiarity of every curve.

"Sinjin . . ." Georgiana began.

"Georgiana . . ." Sinjin began at exactly the same time.

They both stopped and laughed. But Georgiana stopped laughing a bit too quickly.

Looking away from him, she got up and pulled on her shift. Reaching for her corset, she said abruptly, "Sinjin, you may congratulate me. I have accepted a proposal of marriage."

Sinjin blinked a few times and took a deep breath to dispel the tightness that had suddenly formed in his chest. He was glad that Georgiana's back was still toward him. He then got out of bed and, heedless of his nudity, gently turned Georgiana to face him.

"I don't understand. I thought you loved me."

She gave him a sad smile and ran her hands up his well-sculpted chest. "You are so beautifully formed, just like one of those pictures you showed me in your book."

He caught her hands with one of his own and brought her chin up with the other, so that she was forced to look him in the eye.

"I love you," he said, letting the words come up from deep within his soul—to reverberate, hopefully, within hers.

Her eyes filled with tears. "I did not want you to. I did not ask you to."

"But I do." He paused, trying to keep the pain from his voice. "And I thought that you loved me."

"Marriage is not always about love, Sinjin. Sometimes it is about money or social position."

"I have money. Not a lot, but enough."

"Yes. But you do not have a position in society, and you never will."

She pulled away from him, and said, half under her breath, "And . . . you are only nineteen."

Giving one last longing look at his body, she turned to finish dressing. "You should get dressed," she said quietly.

Sinjin just stood there for a minute, unable to move as her words sunk into him.

"If I had a place in society, would you love me?" he asked, impetuously.

"I *do* love you, Sinjin, but I need to marry." She handed him his breeches and shirt from the floor.

"What do I need to do . . . ?"

"You need to get dressed," she said, smiling at him as he stood holding his clothes, but making no move to put them on.

"That's not what I meant."

"I know," she laughed. She had a beautiful laugh and he enjoyed making it bubble from her throat. But now was not a time for laughter.

Now he needed answers. Now he needed to know what he had to do to make her love him as much as he loved her.

He slipped his legs into his breeches. "Georgiana, please, what can I do?"

He pulled his shirt over his head and hastily tucked it in while reaching for his neckcloth.

"There is nothing you can do, Sinjin. Lord Mirthwood has proposed and I have accepted. That is all there is to it."

"But surely . . . what if I gained a position in society? I can, you know, easily. My cousin is the Marquis of Merrick. He can help . . ."

She smiled and turned to help him tie his neckcloth. She always did a much better job of it than he ever did. "Well, if you want to join the beau monde, you should start by caring a bit more about your clothes and how you wear them."

"My clothes are quite fashionable! Why, I bought this waistcoat only last season—and I was assured that it was all the crack."

"Yes," she said slowly, concentrating on what she was doing. "But that was last season. Now the styles are different. You've got to keep up with the times, Sinjin." She reached for his "fashionable" waistcoat and helped him into it. "And really, my dear, all this Latin and Greek . . . well, whoever heard of anyone in society quoting the classics? It just is not done, Sinjin. If you must read it, for God's sake, don't let anyone know!"

He struggled into his coat, once again with her help. Smoothing out the wrinkles, she said, "Sinjin, you are an amazingly handsome man. If you dressed well and made some effort to be fashionable . . ."

"You want me to be a dandy?" he sneered, but the hurt in his voice was close to the surface.

"No, but you asked how you could gain a position in society, and I am telling you."

She reached up and, with tender fingers, brushed back his dark blond hair as it fell over his forehead and into his eyes. Gently kissing his cheek, she said, "Good-bye, Sinjin. Lord Mirthwood and I shall be leaving for America within a few weeks. You won't see me again. Keep well and be happy."

Sinjin just stood looking at her, memorizing every nuance of her face, every movement of her body, and her scent, an unusual musky tone of rose. He caressed her velvety cheek and her thick hair that fell in long chestnut waves around her shoulders. He then bent and feathered his lips across hers ever so gently.

"Adieu, then, my lady fair. Keep my heart well, for it goes with you."

Georgiana's quick answering smile, tinged with regret, lingered with him as he turned and made his way out of the door to her bedroom, careful to keep his shoulders straight as he ran down the stairs.

But by the time he reached the still dark early morning street, his back straightened of its own accord as clear, cleansing resolution flooded him.

He would make himself worthy of her love. He would become just what she wanted him to be.

# 1

*May, 1817*

Rose Grace smoothed her long elbow-length gloves up her arms. And then began twisting her bracelet round and round her wrist. Then she noticed her knee bouncing in front of her.

She stopped the movement of her knee. She was supposed to be behaving like a proper young lady. She sighed; this was not as easy as she had thought it would be.

Once again, she looked about the room, hoping that there would be someone, anyone, with whom she could talk. But not one of the many well-dressed men and women who stood conversing throughout Lady Anson's drawing room were known to her. Her great aunt, who was supposed to be introducing her to eligible young men, sat quietly snoring next to her, her elaborate purple turban having slipped down over one eye.

When they had first walked into the soiree, Rose had felt extremely intimidated by all of the beautifully dressed strangers. But now, after sitting by the side for the past twenty minutes and not speaking to anyone, her anxiety had faded.

It had now been replaced by boredom.

Her attention was caught by a girl who was standing nearby. Rose had been watching her off and on all evening, trying to learn how a young lady behaved. So far, however, all Rose had deduced was that she needed someone to introduce her to other people.

But now she watched with great interest as the girl openly flirted with the man she was speaking with. After giggling delicately at something he said, she batted her eyelashes at him and then gave him a sweet simpering smile. The gentleman looked extremely pleased.

Rose realized that this was how young women attracted men. She supposed she could do that. She quietly stood up and joined her father who was speaking with a number of other gentlemen whom she had not met.

Looking at him fondly, she thought that he looked unusually dashing in his black evening clothes. Then she realized that his neckcloth, which she had helped him with this evening, was coming loose. She giggled to herself, knowing that he would probably not notice this until it came undone altogether.

She did not want to interrupt his conversation, though. Standing unobtrusively next to him, she caught the eye of the middle-aged gentleman facing him. Unlike her father, this gentleman clearly cared about how he dressed. His clothes had a certain flair, despite the sobriety of their colors.

With a little mental shrug, Rose decided to try the tactics of the young women she had been watching, just to see what would happen. Giving a little giggle, she batted her eyelashes at him.

The gentleman raised his thick, graying eyebrows.

Rose gave him a simpering smile.

"Lord Pemberton-Howe!" the man abruptly roared, causing both Rose and her father to jump. "Is this young woman your daughter?"

Rose's father quickly turned toward her. He did not look happy. "Yes, your grace, she is."

"And has she never been taught how to behave in public, sir?"

"Er . . ."

"She has been attempting to flirt with me," the man said, disgust oozing through his voice.

"My daughter?" Lord Pemberton-Howe asked incredulously. "Surely you must be mistaken, your grace."

"Are you questioning my word?" The elder gentleman turned on her father. The color in his face began to rise, as did the volume of his voice. "Perhaps you are unaware, sir, of the position I hold in society?" The gentleman accentuated his words by looking down his nose at Lord Pemberton-Howe.

Rose cringed. Her father was not used to being spoken down to.

"And perhaps you, sir, think nothing of making insinuations concerning my daughter. I will tell you that I will not stand for it!" Lord Pemberton-Howe's voice carried strongly as well.

Rose wished just then that she could have simply disappeared from the scene, but there was nowhere to run or hide. No, she just had to stand there, and hope that her father would not be too furious with her later.

A short burst of laughter interrupted what was quickly becoming a very ugly scene. Quite a few other people who had been standing nearby had turned toward them, eager to hear what the commotion was about.

"My Lord Duke, I believe Miss Grace must have been funning with you," a second gentleman said, a smile still on his face.

Rose now kicked herself for not having looked at the other gentleman present before trying her experiment on the duke. This gentleman was considerably younger, and completely took her breath away.

He was quite a sight. He had numerous watch fobs, as well as a quizzing glass hanging on a bright red ribbon around his neck. His coat was dark blue, and fit him so closely it looked as if it had been painted onto his shoulders. His waistcoat, which was elegantly cut, was a deep red shot through with silver thread, and simply quite dazzling.

But even more remarkable than his clothes was his demeanor. He exuded ennui, speaking slowly, as if he hadn't a care in the world. And yet, Rose felt that behind the bored façade, nothing seemed to pass by him unnoticed.

Rose had never seen anyone dressed so boldly before—it was as if he had taken all of the fashion dictates to another level. Looking at him carefully, she thought he was actually an extremely handsome gentleman, but it was a little difficult to see his face properly behind the ridiculously high points of his shirt.

One thing was clear, however—it definitely should have been him at whom she had been fluttering her eyelashes. Unfortunately, it had been the duke who had caught her eye first.

"Funning? What? Oh, yes. Yes," her father said, turning slightly pink. "That is my little Rose. Always funning. Got quite a sense of humor. She and her sisters."

He shot her a glance that told her she was in serious trouble. Rose gave her father a little apologetic smile in answer and bit the inside of her lip.

The older man's color started to fade back to normal. "Funning you say, Fungy? Harrumph. Well, if *you* believe that's all it was . . ." He grunted in a noncommittal fashion.

"Mind, sir?" the younger gentleman asked Lord Pemberton-Howe.

"What?" Rose's father asked.

"Introduce us?" the man clarified.

"Oh! Yes, of course. Er, the Duke of Argyll, Lord Halsbury, Mr. Fotheringay-Phipps, my daughter, Miss Rose Grace."

The duke nodded curtly to Rose, and Lord Halsbury, a slightly rotund older gentleman gave her a fatherly little smile. But Mr. Fotheringay-Phipps, the well-dressed gentleman who had come to her rescue, took her hand and raised it to his lips, sending Rose's heart fluttering.

And yet, while he was bowing and kissing her hand, his bright blue eyes looked into hers with such amusement and good humor that Rose could not resist smiling back at him. She even felt an answering bubble of laughter springing up from inside of her.

It felt good to unexpectedly have an ally in this strange new world—someone who could understand how odd this all was to her. She just could not believe that the one with whom she felt this empathetic link was this most outrageously fashionable gentleman. But somehow, he was the only one who seemed to understand that this was all a game, and he enjoyed being part of it.

"I am certain that Miss Grace knows she should not flirt with such an esteemed member of society as you, your grace," Mr. Fotheringay-Phipps said, still keeping his mischief-filled eyes on Rose. "But certainly you cannot blame the young lady for trying to liven up an otherwise rather dull affair?"

"Well," the duke huffed, "I must admit this is not the most exciting party I've been to. But really, Pemberton-Howe, you must keep an eye on this one."

"Yes, your grace, I am certain that it will never

happen again. Will it, Rose?" Her father's meaning was clear.

"No, Papa. Please, sir, accept my apologies. I did not mean to be rude or disrespectful. As you said, I am still trying to figure out how one behaves at parties such as this."

The duke nodded. "Well said, Miss Grace. I am certain you have learned your lesson."

Another gentleman standing at the edge of their group gave a little cough. "Er, couldn't help but over-hearing. The younger Miss Grace might benefit from a little lesson like that as well."

Rose's father turned swiftly toward him. "Do I know you, sir?"

"Er, well, no." He held out a delicate white hand, "Haston. Pip Haston."

Lord Pemberton-Howe grasped it hesitantly. This newcomer, judging by his clothing, clearly fancied himself a pink of the *ton*. However, he did not seem very happy to hew to the current style for dark evening clothes—at least judging by his brilliantly colored waistcoat.

His conversational style, however, was less flam-boyant. "Er, met Miss Laia Grace in a shop the other day. Out with her aunt or something. Er, buying rib-bons. Helped her choose the color to match her dress. Got to talking, you know," he said, with frequent breaks to closely examine his shoes.

Rose saw her father nodding his head slowly, un-derstanding, but not quite liking what he was hear-ing. She knew what was coming, and felt a familiar knot of exasperation about her younger sister.

But then, she thought with a wry grin, she had not behaved much better than Laia tonight!

# 2

"Not that Miss Grace was flirting overmuch," Mr. Haston was continuing, his speech more and more hesitant as Lord Pemberton-Howe's face took on an increasingly ruddy hue, "but . . . well . . . might have a word with her."

His voice petered out as he noticed Lord Pemberton-Howe's hands tighten into fists. Rose knew that her father would not create a scene in public, but this piece of information, so soon after her own little exhibition, was clearly proving to be too much for him. She put a restraining hand on his arm.

"How many daughters do you have, my lord?" Mr. Fotheringay-Phipps asked, turning the conversation quickly onto safer waters, as Mr. Haston took advantage of the distraction to disappear into the crowd once more. Rose flashed Mr. Fotheringay-Phipps a quick smile of gratitude.

"Hmm? Oh, er, three. Rose is the eldest. And then there is Aglaia and Thalia."

Mr. Fotheringay-Phipps gave a delighted laugh. "Ah, the Three Graces. Dare I ask if your full name is Euphrosyne, Miss Grace?"

Rose was surprised. She had not thought to expect

this level of erudition from a gentleman dressed as Mr. Fotheringay-Phipps. "Why, yes. As a matter of fact, it is, but I have always been called Rose."

The smile that slowly spread over his face made Rose feel like giggling once more.

Rose folded her fan away and returned his smile. There was something different about this man. She could not put her finger on it, but somehow, despite his dandified appearance, she continued to feel the certain rush of understanding between them. Right away, the evening seemed so much nicer and more interesting.

"Have you been reading Greek mythology recently, Mr. Fotheringay-Phipps?" Rose asked.

"Please call me Fungy, everyone does."

Rose nodded her head, as Fungy continued smoothly, "Shouldn't be too interested in the classics, Miss Grace. Completely understandable since your father is so well known in archeological fields, but not the thing. *The height of cleverness is being able to conceal it.*'"

"De La Rochefoucauld!" Rose's father exclaimed, quite pleased with himself for having figured out the source of the quote.

Rose wished she could be annoyed with Fungy for reprimanding her in public. But he had done it in such a pleasant way that she simply could do nothing but nod her head in acquiescence.

"Young ladies should know nothing of the classics, no matter who her father is," the duke huffed.

Rose was instantly annoyed. She narrowed her eyes, ready to attack, when Fungy interceded. "Ah, but *a woman beautiful in mind as well as in form is a thing indeed to behold.*"

"Who said that?" Rose's father asked.

Fungy gave him a brilliant smile. "I just did."

Rose nearly hit herself in the eye with her fan, as her hand flew up to her mouth to stifle her giggles.

At a quick flick of her wrist, her fan opened and she used it to cover her mouth.

No one had ever said anything so sweet and charming to her! Perhaps this was going to be more fun than she had thought. Even her father looked amused.

"That is an unusual bracelet you are wearing, Miss Grace," Fungy said, holding his quizzing glass to his eye in order to get a better look at it.

"Thank you," Rose said, touching her bracelet. "It was my mother's."

"That is a coin from Macedonia. On its head is Artemis—or Diana, as the Romans called her . . ."

"Papa." Rose put her hand on her father's arm to stop his impromptu lecture before it truly began. "I don't think Fungy needs to hear the entire history of the coin."

"Oh, er, yes, of course."

"But perhaps some other time, my lord," Fungy said, politely.

They were quietly joined at that moment by a rather plain, brown-haired young woman. "Miss Grace, have you met my daughter, Harriet?" Lord Halsbury asked.

"I am very pleased to meet you," Rose said. Although she had been enjoying her conversation with Fungy, meeting another young woman her own age was quite wonderful. So far her sisters were the only other girls she knew, and they really didn't count. It would be nice to make a new friend.

Miss Halsbury was introduced to the other gentlemen, but instead of speaking with them, she turned to Rose. "How are you enjoying your first party, Miss Grace?"

"How did you know that this was my first party?"

"Oh, I was watching you earlier and you looked

rather nervous, so I just assumed . . . But perhaps I am wrong?"

"No. No, in fact, you are absolutely correct. Is it yours as well?" Rose asked, hopefully.

"Oh, no. I am nearly one and twenty. I have been out for years," she said.

"I am the same age, but we have only just returned from Greece," Rose said. She then noticed Fungy being beckoned to by Lord Halsbury, and watched him move away with a sinking heart. She would have liked to have furthered their acquaintance. But she supposed she should be happy to have Miss Halsbury to speak with, and perhaps Mr. . . . Fungy would come back and speak with her some more after he was done speaking with Lord Halsbury.

"It must have been fascinating to live abroad," Miss Halsbury said, trying to reclaim Rose's attention.

Rose, however, was watching Fungy, as Lord Halsbury spoke quietly into his ear and then handed him a card, which Fungy immediately slipped into his waistcoat pocket.

To her surprise, Rose was feeling a void, even as she stood speaking with Miss Halsbury in the midst of dozens of others. Fungy had such an air about him, a vibrancy . . . hopefully he would return soon.

She turned back to Miss Halsbury. What had she asked? Oh yes, living abroad. "Yes, indeed, it was quite interesting, only . . . only I am afraid my mother never had the opportunity to teach me the proper way to go on in society. We lived very quietly just amongst ourselves, and never really met others or had an opportunity to be social."

Sadly, when he was finished speaking with Lord Halsbury, Fungy moved even further away to speak with another young woman and her mama.

"I am certain that you will do quite well, nonetheless," Miss Halsbury said. She too kept her eyes on

Fungy, Rose noticed. She supposed he had the same effect on all young women.

"I hope so," Rose answered. "There seem to be so many things one needs to know in order to go on properly."

Rose watched as the girl he was speaking with smoothed down her dress in such a way that it looked as if Fungy had just complimented her on it.

She found herself smoothing down her own silk dress.

"Fashion is certainly one thing you do not need assistance with," Miss Halsbury said, eyeing her gown.

"Hmm? Oh, I don't know the first thing about what is fashionable and what is not. My sisters and I simply went to a modiste who told us precisely what to have made."

Luckily the high-waisted style that was the fashion was quite flattering to Rose, who was tall and slender. Although Miss Halsbury was not precisely fat, she certainly could not be considered thin either. Her ample bosom seemed to be in danger of spilling out of the top of her dress. All of the flounces at the bottom of her gown gave the impression that she was rather short and squat, which she really wasn't.

"Although," her new friend went on, "your gown is really cut much too high. A lower-cut bodice is much more the fashion."

Rose was certain she meant this in a friendly way. But still the remark made her feel rather self-conscious— perhaps she had erred in insisting that the modiste cut the dress more modestly.

"Er, yes, I know. I just couldn't see myself showing so much," Rose explained, awkwardly. It was not that she didn't have enough to show, it was just that she wasn't used to such a display.

Miss Halsbury gave her a sympathetic smile. "You will get used to it."

Fungy made the girl he was speaking with laugh, and then with a slight bow, moved on to charm the next young lady.

Rose swallowed hard. He probably would not be back after all.


"Rose, it is beyond my comprehension how you could have flirted with the Duke of Argyll!" Lord Pemberton-Howe's voice boomed from across the expanse of his desk. He stood with both hands leaning on the large mahogany desk, which was littered with papers and correspondence. His coat and waistcoat were both unbuttoned and hanging open. If he leaned down just another inch, his silver buttons would thunk against the wood of his desk and perhaps remind him that he had not finished dressing properly.

Rose bowed her head. Her hands were clasped in front of her, and she was biting the inside of her lip. Her father must be truly upset to still be angry about the previous night's incident. She had hoped that he had forgotten all about it, as he had not mentioned it after they got home, but she had been called into the library first thing that morning.

She now absorbed his anger like a sponge, and hoped that all of his yelling would make him feel better so that her punishment would not be too severe.

"You are right, Papa. The way I behaved was wrong, and I am sorry," she said quietly, hoping that a meek reply would soften him. It usually did.

"I have never been so embarrassed. The Duke of Argyll, Rose! He is a strong supporter of the Archeological Society and our work, and a well-respected member of the *ton*. You *must* behave yourself, Rose. Surely your mother taught you how to behave properly in society?"

"Well, no, Papa. How could you ever think that she did? In fact, she told me that it would be best if I stayed away from society altogether. You know that she believed that it is no more than a market for girls to be sold off to the highest bidder—or for married ladies with titled husbands to prove their own importance to those lower on the social scale."

Lord Pemberton-Howe frowned at his daughter, but nodded reluctantly. He then said nothing for a full minute, but stood running his hand through what little hair there was left on his head.

Rose felt a stab of concern. He was looking very tired all of a sudden.

"What is it, Papa?"

He shook his head, and sat down heavily in his leather chair. "I'm afraid I cannot argue with what your mother taught you, but you still need to be more careful about how you behave in public. And, although I have no desire to sell you off, I . . ." He paused and looked pained for a moment. "Please, Rose, you must seriously look about you for a husband."

"What are you saying, Papa?" Rose sat down on the chair just behind her. Her knees suddenly felt too weak to continue to hold her up.

"You *know* that you need to find a husband, my dear."

"Well, yes, but I want to fall in love, just like you and Mama. I want a gentleman to court me, to read poems to me, to go for moonlit walks."

She refocused her eyes back onto her father. "I don't want to get married to just anyone. I want to marry a man I love and who loves me with all of his heart and soul."

Her father gave her a sad smile. "I would wish all of those things for you, my dear, I would. But, unfortunately, we no longer have that luxury."

"I don't understand, Papa." Rose was glad she was

sitting down, for she was beginning to feel oddly light-headed.

"I am sorry, Rose, but you need to marry. Quickly. We do not have the time for you to look for love. You need to marry someone with money, soon. I do not care for a title, but . . . our finances are stretched beyond their limits already, and we cannot continue in this fashion for much longer."

"But surely . . ."

"No, my dear. There is nothing left." He shifted through the papers on his desk. "There is no money coming in from my estate, and I have already spent all that your mother brought to our marriage on our last archeological expedition. That is why we had to return so quickly. There was no money to finish the work. And now . . ."

He paused and picked up a sheaf of bills. Rose recognized them—they were from the mantua makers, the fabric stores and other shops where she and her sisters had purchased all that was needed for their new wardrobes.

". . . Now," her father continued, "we have all of these bills that I cannot pay."

"Not at all?"

He shook his head sadly. "Not one, Rosebud. I simply do not have the money."

"How could there be no money from your estate, Papa? I thought you owned quite a lot of property."

Her father looked a little confused, but shook his head decisively. "I do. But according to these reports from my steward, it is just breaking even. There has not been any profit for many years now."

"And you trust your steward?" Rose had to ask.

"But of course I do! What a question, girl. Strate has been my steward for nearly fifteen years. He is as straight and honest as his name."

Rose nodded. She still didn't like it, but she was beginning to see that she had no option. "But . . . how can I marry without love?"

Her father shrugged. "It is what needs to be done. Nearly all of society does it. You are our only hope now, Rose. Be a good girl and find a nice, wealthy man to marry. Quickly. I know you can do it."

Rose was silent. There was nothing she could say. Nothing she could do, but what her father said, marry soon.

She stood up, feeling as if someone had placed a wooden beam across her shoulders. "I will do the best I can, Papa."

"I know you will, Rose. You are a good girl. I know I can count on you." He placed the offending bills into a drawer.

Rose smiled at this typical action by her father. Hiding them away would not make them go away, but at least they would not be staring him in the face.

# 3

Upstairs in the drawing room, Rose's sisters were eagerly awaiting her verdict.

Laia was sitting with the stitching her great-aunt Farmington had forced on her, her bright red head bowed over the frame. Thalia paced back and forth in front of the empty fireplace, her long legs stretching out in front of her in the most un-ladylike way.

Luckily, it was a warm spring and they had no need for fires, Rose thought as she remembered what her father told her. They would probably not be able to afford the coal even if it became necessary, she thought mournfully.

Or their new clothes. Rose admired Laia's white-and-pink striped muslin dress, and her pink kid slippers that peeped out from just under the hem—they were just the thing for a girl who would be making her curtsey to society in another two years. Thalia's pale green dress, which came down only to just above her ankles, and her brown kid half-boots were also exactly right for an active girl of fifteen. Both their dresses and shoes were new. Along with her own new wardrobe, they would be paid for dearly—as soon as

Rose found a husband who wouldn't mind paying their bills.

"Well?" Thalia asked as soon as she noticed Rose standing in the doorway.

Laia set aside her work. "What did he say? Are you going to be punished?" she asked enthusiastically, as if it were a treat.

Rose came in and sat down on the sofa opposite Laia. "No. But I have to marry. Soon." She tucked a stray dark brown curl back into the knot at the top of her head and then, without hesitation, she related the news of their financial situation to her sisters.

"My goodness!" Laia exclaimed, sitting back against the sofa.

"Oh, but this will be fun!" Thalia said, standing up and away from the mantelpiece against which she had been leaning. Her bright green eyes, which all three girls had inherited from their mother, sparkled with mischief.

Rose and Laia both turned to look incredulously at her.

"What do you mean, fun?" Rose asked.

"I mean, fun." Her adolescent brain was clearly working hard as she thought this out. "We can look through all the gentlemen of the *ton* and pick one out for you. We'll have to find out who is rich, of course, and discount any who are not. And then, we'll discard all the old ones, the ugly ones, and those who are not sportsmen—you can't marry a man who does not love sport, you know." Thalia paused for a breath.

"Thalia, you make this sound . . ." Rose began, but Laia, who was so close in age to Thalia, had caught on to her younger sister's excitement.

"Of course! What an excellent scheme! We'll go to Hyde Park this afternoon and begin our search. It shouldn't be too difficult. I am certain you met quite a few gentlemen already last night, Rose."

"Well . . ."

"Oh come now, don't say that you don't remember their names! I wonder how we can find out who is wealthy enough?" Laia said, thoughtfully poking her needle through her sampler.

"I know! We can look at their horses! A man who is wealthy would not buy a horse without fine points." Thalia threw her long brown braids over her shoulders and then began to pace back and forth again, thinking this through.

"But what if he isn't a good judge of horseflesh?" Rose asked, trying hard not to laugh at her little sister.

"Well, then you definitely should *not* marry him," she said very seriously.

Rose lost control and began laughing. Her sisters were being utterly ridiculous!

"And he should be very handsome. Don't forget that, Thalia. Rose cannot marry a man who is not pleasing to the eye. I think one like those in the friezes Papa found in Greece, with a well-sculpted chest and arms."

Rose laughed even harder. "Oh, yes, definitely. But then, perhaps, I should marry a Greek?"

"But we are not in Greece any more, and surely there have got to be some men like that here."

"Shall I ask the gentleman we choose to disrobe so that I may see his muscles before I marry him?" Rose joked.

Thalia smiled, clearly pleased with the idea, but Laia looked horrified. "You can't ask a gentleman to bare himself!"

"Oh? But I should be sure that he is wealthy, engages in sports, and should judge him by the horse he rides, yes?"

"That's right!" Thalia said.

"Well . . ." Laia was beginning to look uncertain.

"Tell us who you met last night, Rose. Were there any interesting or eligible gentlemen at the soiree?"

Rose became serious as she thought of the gentlemen she had met the previous evening.

"Well, I met your Mr. Haston, Laia, but I don't think he is right for me."

"I thought he was very sweet," Laia said, defending the gentleman.

"Sweet, yes. Intelligent? No."

"Oh well, now you really are becoming quite particular."

"You want him to be smart as well as a sportsman? I don't know, Rose." Even Thalia sounded dubious about finding a gentleman imbued with both of those qualities.

Rose nodded. "Yes, he definitely has to be intelligent. And it would be nice if he had a good sense of humor."

Thalia and Laia had to agree with that.

"And while we're building castles in the air, I think he should be an archeologist like Papa. That would truly be wonderful," Rose continued.

"And he should be romantic." Laia sighed.

"You two are so ridiculous." Thalia scowled at them both. "There is no gentleman who is wealthy, a sportsman, has a good sense of humor, is handsome, is an archeologist and romantic!" she said, ticking off all of the qualities on her fingers. "You might as well give it up right now."

Rose sat back and frowned. Thalia was right. There was no man who would fit that description.

"But she *has* to marry," Laia complained.

Rose shrugged. "Well, I suppose I shall just have to give something up. But let's not worry about that now. Let's first see who my choices are."

"Were there no other interesting gentlemen, Rose?" Thalia asked.

"Only one other young gentleman . . ." Rose said, feeling her face grow warm as she remembered Mr. Fotheringay-Phipps. He was very handsome—and he made her laugh.

"By the look on your face, I would say he was very interesting!" Laia exclaimed.

"Well, there was one gentleman I met who was quite intriguing," Rose admitted. "His name is Mr. Fotheringay-Phipps, but he is called Fungy."

"Fungy!!" Thalia screeched.

Laia frowned. "What sort of name is Fungy?"

"He sounds like a mushroom. Is he?" Thalia asked.

Rose laughed. "No, he is not a mushroom . . ."

"Does he have a big flat head and a tall thin body?" Thalia asked, laughing.

"No! Although he is tall, and rather thin. He seemed well-muscled actually, and looked like he might be a sportsman. But he wore the most ridiculous high collar and an absolutely dazzling waistcoat. Frankly, he looks as if he might be a dandy."

She turned to Thalia, "And, no, my dearest, I do not know what sort of horse he rides, for we were at a soiree and I did not see him arrive or leave."

"Did you ask him what sports he played?" she asked.

"No, I did not. If you meet him, you may do so."

"You can be sure I will."

"So, he is handsome?" Laia asked.

"Yes, tolerably so. He has blond hair, a well-sculpted face, and beautiful blue eyes."

"And is he wealthy?" she said, letting her stitching fall to her lap.

"That I don't know," Rose admitted.

"But wouldn't it be wonderful if he was?" Laia said. "He could be the one—although he does have a rather unfortunate name."

"Well, she can't marry him until *we* meet him and

approve, that is for certain," Thalia said, crossing her arms in front of her.

Both Rose and Laia broke out laughing at her serious demeanor. After wiping the tears from her eyes, Rose said, "I assure you, I will marry no one without your approval, Miss Thalia."

Thalia nodded her head regally and then skipped out of the room.

When they had caught their breath from laughing, Laia said seriously, "Truly, Rose, who *will* you marry?"

Rose sobered up immediately. "I don't know, Laia, but I know that I need to find someone quickly. And if his wealth is all he has to offer, I may need to accept that—for all our sakes."

"You know I would be honored to be the baby's godfather, Merry, but what about Fungy?" the voice of Sinclair Stratton, Viscount Reath, and one of Fungy's closest friends could be heard clearly through the partially open door.

Fungy stopped on the landing just outside the door to his cousin Merry's drawing room. He had not meant to eavesdrop, but it was customary for him not to be announced by Merry's butler. Inadvertently, he had almost walked into this most intriguing conversation.

"Honestly, I'm not sure that he's responsible enough. When it comes to dressing the baby, you know Fungy will be the first person we call. But this is a very important position—and Teresa and I don't want to entrust it to someone who may make a mockery of it. We know that you will take it seriously. We can trust you." Merry's voice was quiet but firm.

At these words, Fungy felt a weight settling in his chest.

Sin sighed. "I appreciate that, and of course, I will be happy to do my best for your son. But when it comes time to release him out into the world . . ."

"Absolutely, Fungy is my man," Merry finished with a laugh. "But until then, Sin, and in everything else, we're counting on you."

Fungy looked down at his impeccable ensemble. Was this all he was valued for—dressing properly?

"And, naturally, Fungy will be able to introduce him to all the right people. Amazing the number of people he knows and socializes with," Sin said, still defending him.

"Indeed. He manages to meet and befriend all sorts. But have you once seen him actually doing anything beyond being social and giving his precious fashion advice?"

Sin laughed. "Must admit, I can't imagine Fungy doing anything actually worthwhile."

"No, neither can I. Don't really think the old boy has it in him," Merry agreed with a chuckle.

Fungy felt the heaviness inside of him blossom into outright pain as these words sliced through his chest. He couldn't take any more of this. He turned and was about to descend the stairs once more when his good friend Julian, Lord Huntley, came bounding up them.

"Ah, Fungy! Thought I'd run into you here," he said, slapping Fungy on the back and propelling him toward the drawing room.

Julian had strongly taken to dressing fashionably ever since he moved to England from his native Calcutta, bonding with Fungy as a mentor and guide in all things fashionable. Now, despite his mixed heritage, he always managed to look more impeccably English than anyone. It was really quite easy at times to completely forget that he wasn't entirely English.

Fungy hesitated, quite desperate to escape. But he had no choice. He squared his shoulders, and entered the room with Julian.

# 4

Fungy saw Sin look quickly away from the door as he entered the room with Julian. Sin pushed a lock of his straight jet-black hair off his broad forehead, revealing his slashing eyebrows which, right now, were pulled low over his eyes. Then he turned away, as if he couldn't meet Fungy's eyes, and helped himself to a cup of coffee from the side table.

Merry, on the other hand, was seated on a sofa looking very relaxed with a sleeping baby in his lap. His coat of blue superfine and pale yellow pantaloons were covered with a soft blanket to protect the baby from the buttons, or perhaps the other way around. Fungy wasn't sure, knowing so little of the creatures. The baby, clearly taking after his father with his fair skin and blond hair, looked rather angelic in his sleep—more like a cherub than the squalling little creature his cousin had described to him two weeks ago, just after the child was born.

"Morning, Sin," Julian said in his normal hearty voice. Then, noticing the baby, he dropped his voice to a whisper. "Morning, Merry."

"It's all right, I don't think anything could wake him when he's sleeping," Merry said.

"Oh. Then why are you watching him?" Julian asked, going over to help himself to some coffee and a slice of the cake that was set out next to the cof- feepot.

"Teresa's asleep, and she still hasn't found a nurse- maid she is happy with." Merry shifted a little under the weight of the sleeping baby. "She had best do so soon, however. Neither of us is getting much sleep be- cause of this little one. He was up half the night want- ing to be fed, changed, burped, and goodness only knows what else. Teresa is running herself ragged, and I can't sleep with all the commotion."

"What you get for procreating," Fungy said, strain- ing to make his voice as light as always. He was having a hard time putting Sin and Merry's disloyal words from his mind.

Sin laughed. "Not something you need to worry about anytime soon, Fungy."

Fungy moved to help himself to some coffee as well, although wishing for something stronger. "Leave that to you three."

"Why don't you get married, Fungy? Rather pleas- ant state to live in," Julian said, before taking a large bite of his cake.

"Had a rather unfortunate experience with love some time ago. Rather not repeat it."

Merry sat up. "You still think about that? My God, that must have been at least ten years ago."

"Fifteen, actually," Fungy supplied.

"What happened?" Julian asked, widening his odd turquoise-colored eyes, which stood out from his honey brown face.

"Fell in love. The lady married someone else, moved to America, and took my heart with her," Fungy answered succinctly, not wanting to dwell on the subject any longer than necessary.

Julian shook his head sadly. "Love is a damned tricky business."

"Indeed."

"But, really, Fungy, don't you think it's time you put that aside and settled down?" Merry asked.

"How about an occupation?" Sin asked, settling his large frame into a delicate chair, since Merry seemed to be taking up the entire sofa himself. "I found serving as a diplomat in India to be great fun, and it put me right in the mood to marry once I returned."

Fungy gave Sin a little smile. He was a good friend, unlike some, he thought, leveling his gaze at Merry. "Thank you, all the same, Sin, quite happy the way things are."

He then turned fully to Merry. "No need to dredge the old heart up out of the muck and mire. If and when I feel the need to set up my nursery, I'll find someone who will not try to, er, engage my finer sensibilities."

Merry just looked at him sadly. Turning to his other friends, Fungy noticed that they too seemed to be regarding him with rather sober expressions on their faces.

"No need to be so glum, old chums! Just because you have all succeeded in filling your hearts with joy, doesn't mean that I need to. Quite happy the way I am, truly."

"It's just a shame, that's all," Sin said.

"Really should try it, Fungy, marriage is . . ."

"My goodness, look at the time!" Fungy said, interrupting Julian. "I've got an appointment with my tailor. Frightfully sorry and all that, got to run." He made for the door as quickly as he could.

If there was one thing he could not stand, it was people feeling sorry for him—and especially not his closest friends.

He was quite happy with his life just the way it was, just as he had told them. There was nothing that he would change, not for an instant, so there was no use even wasting the time thinking about it.

What had hurt him, however, was the fact that Merry and Sin, who had known him for most of his life, seemed to have forgotten what his social mask hid. Was it possible that he himself had forgotten as well?

He had to admit that his run-in the other evening with Miss Rose Grace had sparked something inside of him. It was just a flicker of a reminiscence—of reading and discussing classic texts with his peers at university, of playing with the meanings in the complicated texts they pored over all day and into the night. How long had it been since he'd picked up Plato or Homer or even one of the lighter plays by Euripides, which he used to enjoy so much?

How long had it been since he had truly engaged his mind?

He'd completely given up his passion for the classics long ago, but Miss Grace had made him recall those sweet days of his youth.

And something else as well—a feeling deep within him, long buried—the heat of attraction to a beautiful woman.

"Thank you for the dance, my lord," Rose said, curtsying to the gentleman as he returned her to her great-aunt.

The gentleman bent his tall, thin frame in her direction and then loped off to find his next partner.

"Well, he seems to be a very nice young man, Rose, and I hear he's got ten thousand a year," Aunt Farmington said quietly.

"Yes. It would be nice, however, if he had a brain to go with all that money."

Aunt Farmington glared at Rose. "You are entirely too

fastidious, my girl. You are supposed to be searching for
a wealthy husband, not the man of your dreams."

Rose sighed. It was true. As her father had said, she
did not have the luxury of waiting to find the perfect
man or of giving him time to woo her properly.

"I know. I only wish I could find someone a little
closer to my dream than Lord Simpleton, or whatever
his name was."

Her aunt chuckled. "Stiplton, I believe . . . er, something like that."

Rose couldn't help but laugh, too. Clearly that
gentleman hadn't left a great impression on her aunt
either.

She sobered up quickly enough as she saw Lady
Farmington narrow her eyes at another rather fatuous-
looking young man.

"I had always thought that I would marry a man who
simply took my breath away, the way Mama said Papa
did to her the first time they met."

Lady Farmington snapped her head back to peer
at Rose, her already wrinkled forehead crinkling further with concern.

"And then he would bring me flowers and write
poems to my eyes or some such thing," Rose added
softly, thinking wistfully of the dreams she had had as
a young girl.

"One would think that a girl as intelligent as you
would be beyond dreaming of romantic nonsense like
that," her aunt said caustically.

Rose studied the fan in her hands for a moment and
then gave a little shrug. "It is silly, I suppose," she said,
having to quickly blink to take the stinging from her
eyes. "And it has nothing to do with my current life."

She then lifted her head and placed a smile on her
lips. "Are there any other eligible young men to
whom you could introduce me?"

Her aunt looked at her silently for a moment,

blinking her watery hazel eyes, and then shook her head. Then, her face brightened as she caught sight of another older lady behind her. A rather uncharacteristic smile twitched onto her lips, and she walked slowly over to the lady, who sat in a gilt chair facing the dance floor, her tall feathered turban slowly nodding in time to the sound of the musicians fine-tuning their instruments.

"Mrs. Saxton, how very pleasant to see you again!"

The other lady looked up. "Why, Lady Farmington, what a very pleasant surprise. It has been such a long time since we've had a chat. Do join me."

Lady Farmington took the empty seat next to her and then motioned to Rose.

"My dear, your father is just over there. Why don't you converse with him for a little while? Perhaps he has a young man to introduce to you."

Rose turned to see her father standing by himself next to the entrance to the card room. Turning back to her aunt, she saw that it would now be completely useless to do anything but what she had suggested, for the lady was engaged in deep conversation with her friend.

"Aunt Farmington has abandoned me in favor of a gossip with one of her friends," Rose said as she joined her father.

"What? But . . ."

"Do not worry, Papa, we are merely taking a little break from husband-hunting." Rose sighed heavily. "I am so tired of dancing and being pleasant."

Her father gave a little chuckle. "I must say, I don't believe I've ever seen you behave so well for such a long period of time."

Rose turned to her father, a smile tugging up one corner of her mouth. "What shall we do, Papa? Is there someplace more interesting where we could go?"

Lord Pemberton-Howe raised his eyebrows in mock

surprise. "Euphrosyne, you aren't suggesting that I take my own daughter . . ."

"Oh, all right, how about just into the card room, then? Surely that can't be so bad."

Her father turned and looked a little longingly into that room. He had been planning on slipping in there himself; Rose was sure of it.

She took his arm and gave him a little pull in that direction.

"No, no, my dear, it is not done," he protested.

"What is not done?" Rose feigned ignorance.

"Young girls do not play cards at balls. You should be out here dancing with all the young bucks."

"But I am tired of dancing, Papa. Come, it can't be wrong if I am with you."

Rose saw her father beginning to relent. Her sweet, pleading smile pushed him over the edge.

"All right, but just for a short time, then back to your dancing."

"Perhaps there will be some eligible young men in there you could introduce to me."

# 5

The air in the card room was hazy with cigar smoke. Rose swallowed hard, trying not to cough.

Her father paused to survey the room, and looked around for an appropriate place for them to sit down. The room was filled mostly with men, although there were a few ladies there as well, playing cards and chatting. He led her to a table where two young men were sitting idly chatting and shuffling a deck of cards.

The two gentlemen immediately stood up as Rose moved toward the table.

"Lord Pemberton-Howe. My daughter, Miss Rose Grace," her father said, holding out his hand to the first of the two gentlemen.

"Jack Aiken," a rather ordinary-looking gentleman answered, shaking her father's hand. He was long and thin, as was everything about him. His long face was accentuated by a very long and thin nose. His eyes were small and his hair, which was long and straight, drooped into them. Rose was not at all impressed by his looks, and disconcerted by his deep voice, which was like an ominous roll of thunder from far away.

"This is Lord Kirtland," Mr. Aiken said, pointing to the gentleman next to him.

Now this gentleman, Rose thought to herself, was just the sort to put a girl in mind of marriage and romance. Although not very tall, he was well-built in such a way that Rose could imagine that he might look just like the Greek statues she and her sisters had admired. He was slim, but with powerful-looking broad shoulders, and muscular legs. His finely chiseled chin was strong and masculine, and he had brown, almost black eyes.

"Kirtland? I believe we may have met before," Lord Pemberton-Howe said, shaking his hand.

"Yes sir, at an Archeological Society meeting. I spoke to you last week after your speech on the ruins of Athens."

"Ah, yes, yes. I remember now." Lord Pemberton-Howe smiled and sat down.

"You are an archeologist, my lord?" Rose asked, moving around the table to the other empty chair. Could this be? Could she be so lucky as to have found a handsome archeologist? She was never so glad to have convinced her father to bring her into this room.

Now if he was rich and unmarried, she would truly be in luck. And after the dismal time she had had so far this evening, it was about time that she met someone promising.

"Just a hobby, Miss Grace. I hope someday to make it my occupation. But as yet, I have not had the opportunity to do so."

His dark eyes looked deeply into her own, and Rose felt something like a shiver run up her spine. There was something different, something exciting and dangerous about this man. Rose didn't know what it was. Perhaps it was just the way he seemed to peer so deeply into her eyes that made Rose feel odd and a little unsettled. She sat down abruptly.

Lord Kirtland shuffled the deck of cards in front of him again. "Would you be interested in a game of whist, Miss Grace?" he asked in his soft, smooth voice. Rose firmly set aside her ridiculous and completely unfounded feelings.

"I would, I am certain, enjoy that, only . . . I don't know how to play. Would you be so kind as to teach me the game?" She tried fluttering her eyelashes at him a bit, and was rewarded with a broad smile.

"I would be honored. Aiken, you will be patient for a few moments while I teach Miss Grace the basics of the game?"

"Of course, by all means." Mr. Aiken gave her a small smile and then turned to engage her father in conversation.

The game was simple enough to learn. Everyone placed a card on the table and the highest or the trump card won the trick. They tried playing a few hands just so that she could catch on. When she pronounced herself ready, they added wagering to the game, starting off small, at a penny a point.

Her father was not a very shrewd player. He tended to lose track of which cards had already been played, and at one point even forgot which was the trump. Lord Kirtland, however, was an excellent player and Rose enjoyed matching her wits with his.

After their second hand, Mr. Haston, whom Rose had first met during her uncomfortable interlude with the Duke of Argyll, strolled up to their table. "Ah, my lord, Miss Grace. Pleasant to see you again."

Rose looked up. "Oh, Mr. Haston, how do you do? Would you care to join us?"

"No, thank you. Ain't . . . ain't room at the table," he said, with a small pout that he quickly changed into a little smile.

"Er, please, take my seat," her father said, standing up. "Not very good at this."

"Oh yes, please do take my father's place," Rose begged him sweetly. She was certain she would do much better if she had a different partner than her father. "Don't mind, sir?" Haston said, sitting down. Her father indicated that he did not, then began to let his eyes wander around the room, looking at some of the other games being played.

The next hand was dealt and Rose was happy to find that Mr. Haston was a better player, although he tended to become distracted and make silly mistakes.

As the game went on, the stakes were raised. With a slightly more skilled partner, and her own growing confidence, Rose did not object. With a frisson of pleasure, she noticed that the pile of coins that sat in front of her was growing, rather than shrinking. Although she could hear the music playing in the other room, Rose was very happy to push out of her mind her whole reason for being present at the ball.

She eventually had so many coins in front of her that she wasn't exactly sure what to do with them. With an embarrassed giggle, she simply opened her reticule and let them all slide in.

"You know what this reminds me of, Aiken," Lord Kirtland said, laughing a bit, "that time I won a monkey from old Burncaster and he paid me in coin."

Mr. Aiken gave a small crooked smile, but said nothing.

Rose, however, stopped what she was doing. "You won a monkey? Whatever did you do with it?"

The gentleman began to laugh. "Not a real monkey, Miss Grace," Mr. Haston said.

"A monkey is five hundred pounds," Lord Kirtland explained.

"Oh! My goodness, what a lot of money!"

Lord Kirtland shrugged, noncommittally.

"What would you have done if you had lost?" Rose could not help asking.

"It wouldn't have been a problem, Miss Grace," Lord Kirtland said, giving her a little smile.

"Not for Kirtland," Mr. Aiken added.

"Oh." Rose could say nothing more. The thought of winning or losing that much money was rather overwhelming.

But then she caught her father's eye. It was clear that he was thinking the same as her. While he too was rather shocked at Lord Kirtland's cavalier attitude toward money, that meant only one thing—Rose had to find out if Lord Kirtland was unmarried.

Things were beginning to look better and better.

And they looked even better later that night when Rose had counted all of the money she had won that evening at cards. She had nearly thirty pounds! That was going to be a good start on paying the bills that still sat in her father's desk drawer.

She could barely contain her giggles. What a lot of money to have won!

She sat back on her bed, rearranging her shawl around her shoulders and her shift over her slightly chilled feet, and thought about the evening. Lord Kirtland seemed almost too good to be true. He was an archeologist, handsome, and apparently very wealthy. A few discreet questions by her father had led them to the conclusion that Lord Kirtland was, in fact, unmarried and might very well be interested in changing that in the near future.

There really wasn't much more that Rose could ask for in a husband.

Except perhaps love, her rebellious mind called out.

She shook off that thought. There wasn't time for love. She needed to marry quickly in order to see their bills paid and her sisters taken care of.

Idly running her fingers through the pile of coins, she wondered if she could see a way to play cards again . . .

Rose sat up.

Yes, if she could win money playing cards—enough to pay their bills—then there would be no reason to rush into marriage, would there? If there was not the immediate problem of their bills, then perhaps she could take a little more time to fall in love, or have at the very least a little romance.

She wondered if Lord Kirtland was a romantic man.

# 6

Fungy had nearly reached the docks when he heard a woman scream.

He stopped. These wharfs were no place for a woman. There were all sorts of ruffians around here who wouldn't think twice of taking advantage of a woman alone.

"Help! Oh, Thalia, swim! Please try and swim!" A familiar voice called out from not too far away.

Fungy ran along the road next to the Thames, towards the two women standing at the edge looking out into the ever-crowded water. Ships of all sizes, from large cargo ships to small sailing vessels to small punting boats, warred with each other for space near the dock, some nearly coming close enough to touch.

Fungy stepped up to offer his assistance to the two ladies, when he recognized one as Miss Grace. She stood holding onto the arm of another young lady, who was as slender as she, but had rather wild red hair escaping from her neat little hat.

The two were looking down into the water. Fungy followed their gaze into the choppy, muddy water of the river. For a moment, he saw nothing but a lady's hat. But then a dark head bobbed up to the surface.

"I . . . I'm caught on something!" the girl in the water screamed, a moment before going under again.

A few sailors stopped what they were doing to look, but no one made a move to go in after the girl.

With so many ships anchored, there was a maze of ropes crisscrossing each other in a tangled mess. It was probably in these lines that the young lady had gotten caught.

Fungy looked down at his beautifully polished white-topped Hessian boots and buckskin breeches. He had worn his favorite blue coat and his pale yellow waistcoat with the blue flowers embroidered all over it.

With a sigh, he pulled off his boots and his coat. Then, with a clean move, he dove into the freezing cold, dirty water.

Fungy had always been a strong swimmer, and now he used his powerful arms to carry him to where he had seen the girl surface. The water, however, was so murky that it was difficult to see much of anything underneath.

Taking a deep breath, he dove under the water. As he reached out, his hand touched something slippery and slimy. He didn't even want to think of what it might be. He changed direction, swimming further out into the river. An enormous ship shifted closer to him and he quickly moved out of its way.

Fungy resurfaced and trod water as he thought. She hadn't been quite so close to the ships.

But he had to find her soon—before it was too late to save her.

He heard shouts from the dock. "To your left, Fungy, to your left."

Once again, he turned and searched in the other direction. To his relief, he saw a dark, wet head popping up not too far away. The girl sputtered out water, trying to take in deep breaths of air.

"Miss!" Fungy called out—but she had gone under again.

He took another deep breath and dove under the water, reaching out in front of him. Suddenly, his hand touched something warm. It tried to move away from him, but he grasped it firmly and swam upward. His head and hers came up out of the water at the same time.

"It's all right, I have you," he said as soon as he could. The girl's wide green eyes took him in.

"I wasn't drowning. I'm stuck. My dress is caught on something and I can't tear it away," she said, gasping for breath. "I'm actually an excellent swimmer," she added.

"Well, I'm very glad to hear that. I would suggest, however, that you pick a more secluded spot the next time you decide to go bathing. Or better yet, a private lake in the countryside."

The girl surprised him by laughing. "Thank you, sir, I do believe I shall take your advice. However, I must tell you that I did not intend to go swimming at all this afternoon. I fell in."

"Ah, well, that's a relief. This part of the Thames is not ideal for this sort of activity. Now let's see what we can do to set you free. I don't like all these ships and lines about."

With that, he dove back under the water. Through the darkness, he could see that her white dress was indeed caught on something among all of the ropes which crossed each other deep under the water. She had managed to tear the hem somewhat, so that it hung down lower than the rest of her dress, but it still held her firmly in place. With just another good strong tug it should tear free.

Fungy gave it a try—and indeed the dress came loose. He could feel the churning of the water as she kicked and swam off in the direction of the dock.

Fungy made a move to do the same, but found his own foot caught among the lines. He twisted and pulled, but the ropes only seemed to get tighter the more he struggled.

He was beginning to get desperate for air.

With a great deal of effort, he attempted to calm himself. He was concentrating hard on not moving, when, completely unbidden, a thought came to the forefront of his mind—*really, old man, what have you got to lose?*

Fungy stopped struggling immediately, and instead grappled with this thought. What *did* he have to lose?

He had no family, aside from his parents, whom he hadn't seen or heard from in months. And, of course, his cousin, Merry, who had turned on him only days before, saying that he was feckless and irresponsible. He had no wife, no children . . . who would miss him if he died?

No one.

He had done nothing with his life and had left no legacy. There wasn't even a neckcloth knot or a style of waistcoat named after him.

It would be no great loss to the world if St. John Fotheringay-Phipps was no longer a part of it. He supposed he would be missed momentarily by a few people, but then forgotten like yesterday's news.

Fungy suddenly felt a loosening of the ropes which held his leg. The shifting of the water and the ships above, along with the fact that he had stopped struggling, had freed his foot.

But did he really want to swim up? Wouldn't it be just as well if he stayed here and drowned?

His lungs were beginning to ache with the need for air.

It was his natural instinct for survival that made him kick his legs. Within moments, his head broke through the surface of the water. He gasped in the warm air and then contemplated going under once more, but a voice was calling out to him.

Such a sweet voice it was. One filled with fear and pleading. "Fungy! Mr. Fotheringay-Phipps! Oh, thank God, are you all right? Oh, please answer. Fungy!"

Miss Grace was on her hands and knees at the edge of the dock, leaning over toward the water. Near her was a ladder, at the top of which sat her two sisters. A crowd of onlookers was gathered nearby. A few sailors were peering into the water, but none seemed eager to jump in to save him.

And really, they could not be blamed.

With Rose Grace's lovely face hovering above him, all thoughts of drowning seeped out of Fungy's mind. He swam as best as he could to the ladder and slowly climbed up. Strong hands reached out and got hold of him, pulling him to safety.

His limbs felt like dead weights. If it were not for the help of the sailors, he was not certain he could have made it up entirely by himself. He was set down next to the two ladies, who were evidently Miss Laia and Miss Thalia Grace.

He had the most horrendous taste in his mouth from the dirty water. He leaned over and spat back into the water and then tried to wipe his face dry with his soaking wet handkerchief.

"Oh please, Mr. Foth . . . Fungy, use mine. It is not much drier, but a bit cleaner at any rate." Miss Grace said, handing him the little scrap of cotton and lace that constituted her handkerchief.

It was clear to see that she must have recently been holding onto her recovering sister who Fungy had just saved. The whole front of her sprig muslin dress was soaked through, making the cotton cling quite indecently to her body. Even in exhaustion, Fungy could not help but admire the beautiful Miss Rose Grace.

She handed him his coat and boots, but he immediately handed her back his coat. "Your sister might need this more than I," he said.

"Thank you, but someone has just gone to fetch a blanket for her from a nearby tavern," Miss Grace said, awkwardly holding onto his coat.

"Well, then, I believe you should wear it. The front of your dress is rather wet."

Miss Grace looked down at herself. Her face turned bright red and she quickly slipped her arms into his coat and wrapped it around herself.

Fungy nodded.

Knowing he would ruin his boots if he tried to put them on, he placed them by his side while he caught his breath.

"All roight then, guv'na?" a sailor asked him, leaning his foul-smelling mouth close to Fungy.

Knowing he did not smell too much better after his dip in the water, Fungy forced himself not to recoil. "Yes, thank you. I'll be all right."

"I cannot thank you enough, sir," Miss Grace began, but Fungy held up a hand to stop her gratitude.

"It is quite all right, Miss Grace. Do not say another word." With great effort and a little assistance from Miss Grace and the sailor, he managed to stand up.

The weight of his wet clothes pulled at him, as did the exhaustion that made it difficult for him to move at all. But slowly, he managed to get his limbs moving and walked off, carrying his boots in his hand, to find a hackney to take him home.

"Fungy, please allow us . . ." Miss Grace called after him, but he just walked on, ignoring her. He could not contemplate being social just now, not even with a grateful lady as lovely as Miss Grace.

His mind was filled with all that had just happened, and especially the sobering feelings he had had while caught under the water. He was wet and tired, and it took all of his remaining strength to stay upright. He just wanted to get home.

But most importantly, he wanted to deal with the emotional effect of all that had just happened.

# 7

Rose's heart was still pounding in her chest. First Thalia had nearly drowned in that horrible river and then Fungy. She would not have been able to bear the thought if anything had happened to him while he was saving her sister.

She turned on Thalia, who now sat huddled, shivering, under a rough wool blanket on the ground. She knelt down in front of her and started to vigorously rub Thalia's arms to warm her.

"How could you, Thalia? I have never been so embarrassed in all my life! I can't believe you fell in. If you ever do anything like that again, I swear, I will see that you are punished so severely . . ."

"Rose!" Laia exclaimed, moving to sit up on her knees.

"But it was an accident." Thalia defended herself at the same time.

"It was an entirely avoidable accident," Rose said, looking around to make sure there was no one eavesdropping on their conversation. Luckily, this area of the dock was mostly empty, the officers and sailors from the ship moored nearby having all left.

"No, don't you defend her either, Laia, because this

is equally your fault," Rose said, turning back to her sisters. "I saw the way the two of you were fooling around, jumping in front of each other while I was trying to get information about the ship bringing our things from Greece."

Laia and Thalia sat quietly, looking at her from under their eyelashes. They both looked so contrite that, for just a moment, Rose felt her heart softening. But she quickly snapped back to the reality of the situation.

"Don't look at me like that. I know full well what you are doing, and I am not Papa to be fooled by your sorrowful eyes. I taught you that trick, so it is not going to work with me."

"But Rose, it truly was an accident," Thalia complained. "I assure you, I had no intention of falling into that disgusting water."

Rose frowned and looked at the swirling brown water of the Thames next to them. "No, I am certain that you did not. However, if you two hadn't been playing your silly game, whatever it was, then none of this would have happened."

"But it wasn't a silly game," Laia said.

"Well, Laia was trying to get a look at the sailors . . ."

"The officers," her sister interrupted.

"All right, the officers, on that ship and I was trying to stop her. You and Mama have said in the past that she shouldn't ogle men."

Rose turned to Laia, who had the grace to blush.

"Well, I . . ."

"I don't want to hear any more of this. Laia, I think you will be staying at home for the next three days until you learn to control yourself."

"But, Rose!" Laia objected.

"Not another word or else I will tell Papa what has occurred and let you see what sort of punishment he thinks is appropriate."

Laia opened and closed her mouth a few times, and then finally settled on a pout.

"I don't see why you're so angry, Rose," Thalia said quietly. "There was no harm done, if you don't count the loss of my hat and this dress—I didn't particularly like this dress anyway."

"What do you mean, no harm done!" Rose nearly shouted, moving to her feet. "What about Fungy? What about the fact that both you and he nearly drowned? You didn't see how long he was under the water after he tore your dress free. I thought he was never going to come up again."

Laia and Thalia both looked at Rose in great surprise.

She swallowed the sob that tried to break free from her throat. "He nearly drowned saving you, Thalia," she said hastily, wiping the tears from her cheeks.

"Rose, I am so sorry. I didn't know."

"You really like him." It was more of a statement than a question, but Laia was looking at her with wide eyes.

Rose sniffed. "No! I mean, well, I don't know the man, do I? We've only met once. But he was very kind to me when I met him, and he got me out of an awkward situation. And now he has risked his life to save Thalia." She crossed her arms over her chest, feeling the soft wool of Fungy's coat under her fists.

Her sisters just looked at her. Rose began to feel uncomfortable—as if they were trying to read her mind. Since she, herself, didn't know what to think about these strange feelings running through her, she quickly turned away.

"Come, let's see if we can't find a hackney to take us home."

As she had decided just the previous night that Lord Kirtland was the most eligible man she had yet met, she could not figure out why she was having all these strange feelings about Fungy. She could never marry a dandy, and she had no idea what his financial situation was. No, she should put all thoughts of Fungy directly out of her mind.

But his torso and arms had looked truly magnificent in his nearly transparent wet shirt. There would be no need to ask him to bare himself for her to inspect his muscles. He had practically done so already.

The girls were silent for most of the ride back to their rented house on Soho Square. The hackney was dirty and smelled—or perhaps that was Thalia. Rose couldn't tell the difference. But it was not an altogether unpleasant ride, despite the open windows.

Finally, Thalia asked, "Why do you think he left so quickly?"

Rose just looked at her, amazed that her sister should be thinking exactly the same thing that had been going through her own mind. She swallowed hard and shook her head. "I don't know."

"He seemed rather rude. I mean, I know he had just saved Thalia's life, but you would think that he would have done the gentlemanly thing of seeing us home, or at the very least into a hackney to take us home." Laia had clearly been thinking about this as well.

"I suspect he was just cold and tired," Rose said, although she didn't know why she should defend him. It was true that he had been a bit rude.

They arrived home just at that time, so Rose was spared thinking about this any further.

"Miss Thalia! Miss Grace! What happened to you?" Reynolds, the Graces's butler, exclaimed loudly as they came into the house.

Three hands went up. "Shhh! Papa will hear!" they whispered fiercely.

But it was too late. Lord Pemberton-Howe threw open the library door and caught the girls before they could even move toward the stairs.

"What is this? What has occurred?"

"Nothing, Papa," Laia said immediately.

"It is all right, Papa. Thalia just had a little accident, but she is fine," Rose said, trying to push her youngest sister toward the stairs before her father could see the state of her dress and hair. But it was too late for that too.

"Rose! Whose coat is that you are wearing? And Thalia! My girl, what happened? Reynolds! Hot water, quick."

"Oh yes, Reynolds, Thalia is going to need a bath right away," Rose said, ignoring her father's questions.

"I am already on my way, Miss Grace," the butler said, slipping past them all on his way to the kitchen.

Lord Pemberton-Howe moved to get a closer look at his youngest daughter. Immediately, his hand went up to his nose. "Oh, my dear, the stench! And you are soaking wet."

"I, er, fell into the river. But I am perfectly fine. I swim quite well, only . . ."

"Only?"

Thalia looked down at the puddle she was making on the floor. "Only my dress got caught on something and a gentleman had to jump in to save me."

"He was so brave, Papa, and handsome, even soaking wet," Laia gushed.

"What? Who was this gentleman? Did you get his name?"

"It is perfectly all right, Papa. It was Mr. Fotheringay-Phipps, whom we met the other night," Rose said, giving Laia a quelling look. "Now, please, Papa, Thalia should not stand here any longer. We must get her out of those clothes and into a hot bath."

"Oh, yes, yes, of course." Her father backed away, allowing the girls to pass by him in the narrow hall. Before they got to the top of the stairs, however, he called up, "Rose, I would like to see you in the library as soon as may be."

"Yes, sir," Rose answered with a sigh, before following Laia up and to the room she shared with Thalia.

She had hoped that her father wouldn't find out about this little adventure. It was difficult enough taking care of her younger sisters, but to have to explain everything to her father as well . . .

If only he didn't worry so, she thought. But years of experience of dealing with Rose and her sisters had taught him well—they may be girls, but they did rather have a penchant for getting into trouble.

Rose quickly saw Thalia into the bath and then left her to the care of Laia and their only maid.

Entering her own room, Rose felt like doing nothing more than collapsing into her own bed. But she was still wet, from having clasped her sister to her after she had been pulled from the river, and her father was waiting for her downstairs.

She slowly pulled off Fungy's coat, and then could not resist the temptation of smelling the warm wool. It smelled so much like him, musky and clean. It was a lovely smell, though just now it was a bit tinged with the smell of that awful dirty river. She carefully folded the coat, to be returned later, and set it aside.

Quickly divesting herself of her own dirty muslin dress and underclothes, she bathed herself in the mug of warm water she had taken from her sister's clean bath.

It was turning out to be much more difficult to watch out for her sisters than she had anticipated. She had always known that her mother had, at times, wanted to tear her hair out at the girls' tomfoolery.

But she had never realized how much worrying was a part of caring for someone.

She loved her sisters dearly, however, and she would

continue to do her best in spite of their efforts to get into trouble. But really, it was past time that they learned to behave like proper young ladies.

Rose had to think about this. It was not too long ago that she would have thought this the greatest lark—aside from the fact that Fungy and Thalia had nearly drowned. But somehow, now that she was the one responsible, it no longer seemed so much like fun. Now she saw how inappropriate such behavior was and why. If she and her sisters were to marry well, they could not afford for society to see them behaving this way. It was not right.

Just the thought of that sent a chill through Rose. Her mother had never strongly reprimanded Rose or insisted that she behave herself when she was Thalia's age.

But now, she knew that she was seriously lacking in her social education. She would have to see that her sisters did not have the same problems as she did when they became old enough to make their debuts into society.

Rose stopped in the middle of tying her corset. In less than two years, Laia would be old enough to make her come-out. Already she had more than a healthy interest in men. Rose did not just need to marry a man who was wealthy, but preferably one who had a mama or older sister who could oversee the girls' social education and entrance into society.

Rose resumed tying her corset. She was just pulling a clean dress over her head when there was a little knock and Laia walked into the room.

"Rose? I just wanted to apologize for my behavior earlier," she said quietly.

Rose turned and gave her sister a hug. "It is all right, Laia. Here, help me with my buttons."

She turned her back to her sister, so that she could button up the back of her dress.

"Life was so much easier when we had more maids," Laia said, trying to change the subject.

Rose would not allow it, however. "Laia, I know it is difficult to behave properly sometimes. But really, you must try to restrain yourself. You are old enough now to know better."

Rose sat down in the chair at her dressing table and began pulling the pins from her hair.

Laia stood behind her and picked up Rose's hairbrush. "I know. It is just that sometimes I forget. And the officers on that ship looked so handsome in their uniforms . . ."

Rose gave her sister a little smile in the mirror. It was sometimes difficult not to enjoy watching handsome men dressed in uniforms, she thought to herself while enjoying the feeling of her long dark brown hair being brushed. "And how typical of you to notice, even from that distance."

Laia gave a guilty giggle. "You are certainly not going to tell me that you did not notice how well Fungy looked after he climbed out of the water?"

Rose felt herself color. "Well . . ." She fiddled with her hairpins on the table in front of her.

"I saw the way you looked at him . . . And the way he looked at you—in your nearly transparent dress before you put on his coat."

"Laia!" Rose saw her own cheeks flush bright red in the mirror.

"But he is very handsome. And he was so brave to jump into the river to save Thalia. You are so lucky, Rose, to have found a husband so quickly!"

Rose looked up at her sister's reflection and swallowed hard. "What do you mean? I have not found a husband."

"But Fungy . . ."

"I am not going to marry him, Laia," Rose said, ignoring a little feeling of sadness that came over her as she spoke the words.

"Why not? He may have been a little rude, but as you said, he was probably just tired and wanted to go home to change." Laia put the last pin into place to hold up the simple knot into which she had twisted her sister's hair.

Rose thought about Fungy, and tried to put her misgivings into words.

"It is true that he is a very kind man, and for what he did today I shall forever be in his debt, but . . ." Rose got up from her dressing table and walked slowly across the small room toward the door. "But he is a fashionable dandy. He is all posturing and airs—more concerned about how he looks, and how he is perceived by others, than about anything else. I am not at all certain that he engages his mind very much, if at all. Truly, I could not marry a man like that."

*Not when there was Lord Kirtland to compare him to.*

"You would prefer someone more intellectual, like Papa?"

Rose turned back to her sister and smiled, "Yes. And besides, we don't even know what sort of fortune Fungy has."

Rose smiled at her sister. "Anyway, even if I decide on Fungy, or anyone else, there is the small problem of making sure that *they* would want to propose to me, isn't there? Anyway, now, I must go down and face our father before he wonders what has become of me."

# 8

Rose slowly made her way down the stairs, her mind churning with thoughts of Fungy, Lord Kirtland, and her need to marry quickly. She did wonder what sort of fortune Fungy had. There must be a way to find out.

Of course, she wouldn't need that information if she decided to marry Lord Kirtland. He, she was certain, was quite wealthy. Why, someone who could stake five hundred pounds in a card game had to have quite a fortune.

She knew she could never even dream of winning so much. However, she did hope to have the opportunity of winning at least enough to cover their bills. She just had to find a way to do so.

She wondered if she could ask her father to bring her into the card room at the next ball they went to. If not, she supposed she could ask Lord Kirtland if he knew of a way for her to play cards again.

She paused just inside her father's study. He was standing with one foot on the fender, staring into the empty fireplace, a drink in his hand. She noticed that he was wearing his old breeches, and a slightly shabby though serviceable brown coat. His boots had seen better days—although she was sure Reynolds, who was now acting as his lordship's valet as well as their butler, had done the best he could with the old things.

No, she could not ask her father for help. He had enough troubles on his shoulders already. It would have to be Lord Kirtland to whom she would turn.

Lord Pemberton-Howe turned around with a start. "Oh, Rose, I did not hear you come in."

He gestured for her to sit down on the dark green sofa, but stayed standing by the fireplace himself.

"I want to know precisely what occurred at the docks, Rose," her father said in his most serious manner.

"It was an accident, Papa, just as we told you. Thalia just leaned a little too far out over the water and fell in," Rose said, modifying the truth just a bit so that her father would not worry overmuch.

Her father looked at her searchingly. It was clear, however, that he knew that there was more to the story than she told him.

Finally, he sighed and said, "Very well. I am certain you are doing your best to watch after your sisters. I know your mother constantly worried about the tricks the three of you got up to. But you know your own sisters, and I trust you to look after them. It is not easy, but I know that you will do the best you can."

Rose did not say a word. She could not bear to let her father know how worried she was about having this responsibility. He already had enough to be anxious about. She could not impose her own misgivings on him as well.

Looking as strained as he had the last time they had talked in the library, her father sat down on the sofa next to her. Rose felt a rush of warm affection and concern for her impractical yet brilliant father. He was trying so hard to be a good parent to her and her sisters. It had not been easy since her mama had died over a year ago.

Putting a comforting hand on his arm, she said, "It will be all right, Papa."

He nodded and patted her hand. "It is not so easy for a man such as I to raise three girls by myself. But I know I can count on you to help me."

He then turned to her and gave her a sly smile. "Now tell me about Fungy."

Rose just shook her head and laughed.


Fungy surfaced from the deepest sleep, slowly coming to consciousness as he had swum up from under the surface of the river.

He sat up with a start and took in a deep breath of air.

It was all right. He was in his own bed. Only his covers were tangled around his legs, just like the rope which had held him under the water. Quickly, he pulled them free, throwing back the blankets and reveling in the feel of the cool air on his bare legs.

The murky light of the waning day seeped in through the mostly closed drapes in front of his window. Fungy's stomach rumbled with hunger.

Donning his dressing gown, he found his valet, Thomas, in the small kitchen making an attempt at saving his waistcoat from the rubbish heap.

Fungy always felt like Gulliver in the land of the Lilliputians whenever he walked into the little kitchen that was Thomas's kingdom. Everything was small, even the dapper valet, who stood a full foot shorter than him.

Thomas looked up as he entered the room. "It may be hopeless, sir. Even if I got all the dirt off, the stench would be sure to linger. And the embroidery is so delicate that I would be afraid it would be quite ruined were I to attempt to wash it."

Fungy caressed the waistcoat like an old friend,

but then handed it back to the valet. "Do not bother with it anymore, Thomas. Simply throw it away."

The man slouched forward for a moment in resignation, but he quickly regained his erect posture, and sighed, "Yes, sir."

He folded the destroyed garment and put it out of sight.

"I am famished. Is there anything to eat?"

"Certainly, sir. If you would wait for just a few moments in the drawing room, I will bring out a cold collation of meat and cheese."

Fungy nodded and went back out to the drawing room—where everything was once again of a normal size. He sat down in his favorite chair by the fire, next to which stood a table littered with the day's newspapers, all opened to the gossip pages. There were also a couple of books, lying facedown to hold the pages where he had stopped reading. He had searched through his old trunks a few days earlier, and found a gold mine of all his old favorite books.

Idly, he picked up Socrates's rendering of Plato's *Apology*. But deciphering the original Greek was too much of an effort just now. He was sure it would come easily to him once again, but he needed a bit more practice.

Tossing it back onto the table, he reached for a newspaper, and turned it back to the front to read what was happening in the world around him.

Thomas came in with his food, and Fungy ate and read in silence—until the unbidden thoughts that had haunted him while under the murky depths of the Thames slid into his consciousness once more.

*No legacy. No wife or children. No occupation. What had he done with his life? Who will remember him when he's gone?*

The words echoed over and over in his mind. In desperation, Fungy jumped up from his chair and strode to the window. There must be some way to shut out these nagging voices. He leaned his fevered head against the cool glass of the window, and closed his eyes.

And there she was. Rose Grace. Her face hovered above him, looking so worried and fearful as she called out his name, begging him to return to the dock.

She really was quite lovely. It had been absolutely impossible to look up into that face and then consign himself to the depths of the river.

Fungy opened his eyes and looked out into the street. People walking by, carriages carrying ladies home from their shopping expeditions drove past— an ordinary day for most, and yet such an extraordinary one for him.

A sudden knock on the door jarred Fungy out of his pensive mood. He waited and heard another man's voice in the hall. And then Julian, Lord Huntley, entered the room, looking ready for the evening in his dark blue coat with a pair of matching pantaloons.

"Hello, Fungy. I hope you don't mind me dropping by. I just wanted to see how you were doing."

Fungy took his friend's outstretched brown hand and held it in a firm grip for perhaps a moment longer than usual.

"You are all right, aren't you?" Julian asked, now with a worried tone to his voice.

"I shall come about, I suppose." Fungy turned around and noticed the rest of his meal still spread out on the table. "Care for something to eat?" he offered.

"No, thank you. I'm off to Whites for dinner in a bit. How is it that you're not dressed? Are you sure you are all right?"

"What?" Fungy looked down at the maroon brocade dressing gown he was still wearing. He hadn't even bothered to put any slippers on his feet, preferring the feel of the solid wood floor beneath his toes after the dreadful memory of his dip in the water that morning.

"Er, yes! Quite all right. Come along then, and keep me company while I dress."

Julian followed him to his bedchamber, and then settled down on a chair while Fungy randomly pulled clothes out of his drawers and wardrobe.

Julian sat up, watching him closely. Fungy noticed that his blue eyes were now full of concern, and wondered how much he could unburden himself.

"What has happened this morning, Fungy? What is wrong?"

Fungy randomly tossed a dark green coat on top of the pale blue pantaloons on his bed and then sat down on both of them, heedless of the creases it would cause.

"I have realized that you and Sin were right, Julian," he said. "I need to do something. To marry, have children . . . perhaps Sin's idea of an occupation was the right one. You know, *o de anexetastoz bioz ou biotoz anthropo.*"

"I'm sorry, Fungy, *what* was that you said?"

Fungy gave a little laugh, and translated. "*The unexamined life is not worth living.* Sorry, old man, I'm reverting to old habits. It's Greek."

Julian laughed in turn. "I see. They didn't teach us Greek in Calcutta. If you need an appropriate quotation in Bengali, though . . ."

Abruptly, Fungy held up his hand to stop his friend from speaking. There was something nagging at his mind.

In a snap he had it. He jumped up and opened the door, calling for his valet.

The man came at a run. "Yes, sir."

"Thomas, there was a card from a Lord Halsbury in the pocket of my waistcoat, the one I wore to Lady Anson's soiree . . ." Fungy began.

The man nodded and immediately went to his

shaving table and pulled a card from one corner of the mirror. "You mean this one, sir?"

Fungy took it. "Yes. Indeed, this is the one. Thank you, Thomas."

The man nodded and then went to straighten the clothes Fungy had tossed onto his bed. He shook out the blue pantaloons and then offered them to his employer to put on.

"So, you are going to start looking about for a wife?" Julian asked, hesitantly.

"Yes." Fungy stopped to button his pantaloons. "I actually did meet a fascinating young woman, Miss Rose Grace."

"I don't believe I know her," Julian said.

"Extremely intelligent. Father is the famous archeologist Lord Pemberton-Howe. Just back from Greece."

"I've never thought of you as fancying the bluestocking sort."

"And there is also Miss Halsbury—you know, the Parliamentarian's daughter. Very sweet girl," Fungy said, mentally going through all of the young ladies he'd met recently.

"I've met her. Rather quiet, isn't she?"

Fungy reached for the neckcloth Thomas was offering him.

"Yes," he said, as he tied a simple knot in the starched linen.

He then paused for a moment, before slipping his arms into the waistcoat Thomas was holding out for him. Thomas was about to return the green coat to the wardrobe, but Fungy absently took it from him. As the valet began to protest, Fungy continued, "Can't think of anyone else who has caught my eye recently. Imagine there will be more if I look about."

"Yes." Julian tilted his head to one side. "Er, Fungy, that coat with those pantaloons . . . ?"

Fungy had just slipped his arms into the coat and taken a look in his mirror. He frowned at his reflection.

"Won't do at all, will it?" he said with a little laugh.

Julian burst out laughing as well. "You are a cad! You nearly had me going there!"

Fungy gave his friend a rueful smile. He shook off the coat and gave it apologetically back to Thomas.

He really needed to watch himself if he wanted both to attract a young lady and keep his friends from worrying overmuch. Luckily, Julian had just thought that he was funning.

But in fact, he had not been watching, or caring about what he was doing. It was very unlike him. But again, it was not every day that one nearly died and had to completely reprioritize one's life.

# 9

"How kind of you to call, my lord," Rose said as she sat back down on the dark red-and-white striped sofa of the drawing room. Lord Kirtland took the seat opposite her in the matching chair.

Clasping her hands together tightly in her lap, Rose tried to calm herself. She desperately wished that Laia was next to her to support her in what she had to do, but she was across the room with Aunt Farmington hovering over her, gaily entertaining the two other gentlemen callers. And besides, Rose had not yet told her sisters about either Lord Kirtland or her gambling.

*But at least Lord Kirtland had finally come!* She had been so afraid that he wouldn't visit, especially after quite a few of the other gentlemen she had met the other night had already come and left that afternoon. But Lord Kirtland was the only one she truly wanted to see, and he had been the very last one to call.

Rose had had a difficult time sitting still and being polite to all of the people who had visited. All day, she had jumped up each time another guest arrived, but now, finally, he was here.

Rose took a deep breath. Now for the next step. How

could she bring card-playing into the discussion, and dare she introduce it into the general conversation?

No, she quickly decided. If she was going to find out where to play cards, she had to speak to Lord Kirtland privately. She remembered what her father had said—how it was inappropriate for young girls to want to play cards and gamble.

But it was essential that she resolve it this afternoon.

"I was disappointed to find you not at home yesterday, Miss Grace," Lord Kirtland was saying, as Rose handed him a cup of tea.

Rose looked at him appreciatively. He was looking as handsome as ever, neatly and fashionably dressed, but still causing her little shivers every time he looked at her with those disquietingly dark eyes. "Oh, my sisters and I had gone to see about our household goods, my lord. They are being shipped from Greece. Unfortunately, the ship has not yet arrived."

Rose placed a smile on her face, trying to hide her anxiety. This was going to be difficult. Bound by convention, she was forced to sit and make polite conversation, but it was certainly the most arduous exchange she had ever had.

However, as her sister and aunt were at the other corner of the room with the two other callers, Rose and Lord Kirtland were sitting quite by themselves. She wondered if she dared to quickly change the subject while she had the opportunity.

Before she could continue however, Lord Kirtland replied easily, "I am sorry to hear that. I hope that it arrives soon. May I ask if you have brought back any interesting artifacts from your father's expeditions?" he asked, sitting back comfortably with his tea and completely unaware of her tension.

"Oh, no. The most significant objects were immediately handed over to the government. Unlike Lord

Elgin, my father does not believe in stealing precious artifacts from Greece."

"Old Lord Elgin *stole* the marbles?" Lord Strapton asked dimly, arranging his lanky limbs in the spindly chair next to Lord Kirtland. He was followed by Laia, happily leaning on the arm of young Lieutenant Wroughtly, with her aunt quietly bringing up the rear.

Rose groaned silently. She had lost her opportunity.

But Lord Kirtland had also seized upon Rose's statement. His voice rising slightly, he proclaimed, "Lord Elgin did *not* steal the marble relics from Greece, Miss Grace. He *rescued* them."

Now this was a topic in which she felt absolutely confident. Rose felt her nails bite into her palms, as her temper flared at his tone. She knew that this was a very touchy subject among archeologists, but it was one that she and her family felt very strongly about.

She worked hard to keep her tone moderate and polite. "That is what he claims, my lord. However, there are others in the archeological society who feel . . ."

"Oh, in the archeological society!" Lord Strapton said, with a dismissive air—not, Rose thought, that he knew anything about the society at all. "Well, of course, *they* would hold odd views about the subject."

Lord Kirtland frowned at the gentleman. Clearly, he too knew that Strapton was totally ignorant about the subject. "There are differing viewpoints even within the archeological society, Strapton. And I believe that Lord Elgin should be commended for saving the marbles from falling further into ruin, and be rewarded handsomely for doing so."

Rose heard Laia gasp, and immediately put her hand on her sister's knee while simultaneously biting back her own sharp retort. While she would have dearly liked to have engaged Lord Kirtland in an argument on the topic, this was not the time—she needed him too badly just now to alienate him in any way.

"Miss Grace, do you plan on attending Lady Yarborough's soiree tomorrow night?" Lieutenant Wroughtly asked. Rose threw him a grateful look, while also worrying about how besotted Laia was looking as she too turned toward the gentleman. However, to his credit, he had wisely stayed out of the argument, and for once his polite, meaningless conversation was exactly what was needed.

"I had rather hoped that she would attend Mrs. Cartwright's rout, don't you know, so that I might have another opportunity to dance with her," Lord Strapton said, giving Rose his usual charmingly vacuous smile.

"I am deeply flattered, gentlemen, truly I am. But my aunt and I have not yet decided which party we shall be attending tomorrow. Have we, Aunt Farmington?"

"No, my dear, actually I was thinking that we should try to pay our respects to both hostesses."

"Oh, but Mrs. Cartwright's routs are really quite out of the ordinary," Lord Strapton said with conviction.

"Not any more so than Lady Yarborough's soirees," the Lieutenant argued.

This was the opportunity Rose had been waiting for.

While the two men carried on their good-natured argument, with Laia and Lady Farmington proffering their opinions, Rose turned back to Lord Kirtland and said quietly, so that only he could hear her, "My lord, I was actually hoping that you would know of some place where I might go to play cards once again. I must admit that I truly enjoyed myself the other evening."

He leaned forward so that they might have a more private conversation. Unfortunately, his discreet words were not what Rose wanted to hear.

"I am happy you enjoyed our little game, Miss

Grace. However, it is not strictly proper for a young lady to play cards."

He reached forward and helped himself to a slice of cake. "In fact, I was quite surprised that your father brought you into the card room at Lady Bascombe's ball. It is quite unusual for a young lady to play cards at a ball. They are much more likely to be found dancing."

"Oh, well, I did dance quite a bit that evening. I had grown tired, however, so my father was kind enough to offer to escort me into the card room," Rose said, fudging a little on the details. She was not sure how Lord Kirtland would react if she told him that her father had only brought her into the card room for a lark—he might very well be a rather straight-laced gentleman who stuck to the rules.

Kirtland gave a nod, his mouth too full of cake to comment.

"But is that the only place where I could play?" Rose persisted.

Kirtland took a sip of tea. "I am actually attending a card party on Tuesday evening, hosted by Lady Kemble. But again, I do not believe that it is at all proper for a young lady such as yourself to attend."

Lord Strapton interrupted their quiet conversation by coughing obviously. The gentlemen's argument had clearly been resolved, and he was ready to leave. As he stood up and made his parting comments, Rose stood as well and walked him to the door of the room. "Thank you so much for coming, my lord."

"Thank you, Miss Grace. May I be assured of a dance tomorrow evening at the rout?"

"Yes, of course, my lord, if we decide to attend that party, I shall certainly be happy to meet you there," Rose said easily. Even if he was not the most interesting man she had ever met, and held rather odd ideas about archaeology, at least she would not be a wall-flower the entire evening.

"Oh, and though it may not be strictly proper, there is going to be a masquerade at Vauxhall Gardens next week . . ."

"Absolutely not!" her aunt said firmly from behind her.

Rose gave a little giggle and a shrug. "It was a good try, my lord." It was such a shame that Aunt Farmington knew her so well. There surely could be nothing more fun than a masquerade.

The young man looked a little taken aback by her aunt's forcefulness and left quickly. An idea, however, was quickly forming in Rose's mind.

She went back to Lord Kirtland, who was finishing off his cake. They still had some privacy, since Laia was flirting with the dashing young officer, and Aunt Farmington had returned to her side in order to keep a sharp eye on the proceedings.

"My lord," she said quietly, refilling his cup of tea, "what if I attended the card party in a domino? That way no one would know who I was."

Lord Kirtland thought about this for a moment, nodding his head. "I have known ladies to do so in order to maintain their anonymity. Of course, you would need a gentleman to vouch for you . . ."

Rose batted her eyelashes at Lord Kirtland, and began to try to think of other ways she might convince him to take her, if that didn't work.

But it did not seem necessary, for although he looked for a moment as if he might say no, he relented at her sweet, pleading smile.

He returned her smile. "Very well, Miss Grace, if that is what you truly wish to do?"

"Oh yes!" she said quickly.

"I am not at all sure . . ."

"Oh please, my lord?"

He stole a look at her aunt.

"I assure you, no one need know," Rose said.

He nodded. "Then I shall be honored to take you—if you wear a domino."

"Oh thank you, so very much, my lord. I truly do appreciate it."

Rose had a hard time not bouncing in her seat, she was so excited. Everything was working out exactly the way she had hoped.

# 10

After Lord Kirtland and Lieutenant Wroughtly had left, Rose went to her room to rest in preparation for her outing to the opera that evening. Her sisters, however, invaded her room not two minutes after she had lain down on her bed.

"What was it that you and Lord Kirtland were whispering about?" Laia demanded.

Thalia looked expectantly at her sister as well.

"Oh, we were discussing something that occurred at Lady Bascombe's ball the other night," she said as innocently as she could. But as she expected, it was not enough for her overly curious little sisters. And in fact, Rose had to admit that she wanted to share her excitement with them as much as they wanted to hear everything that she did.

She sat up on her bed and gestured for her sisters to join her. "Well, after I had danced for some time, Aunt Farmington found an old friend of hers and fobbed me off onto Papa. I told him that I was bored with dancing, so he was kind enough to bring me into the card room with him. It was there that I met Lord Kirtland and a friend of his, Mr. Aiken. They taught me how to play whist and . . ."

She paused for effect, and then, smiling at their rapt faces, continued, " . . . and I managed to win nearly thirty pounds!"

Thalia gasped, while Laia's pale green eyes began to sparkle with excitement. "You won? I can't believe . . ."

"Why can't you? Our sister is extremely intelligent. Why shouldn't she win at cards?" Thalia said, suddenly very defensive.

"There is no reason why she shouldn't. But I'm just surprised that she did," Laia said. She then turned back to Rose. "So that is what the two of you were talking about?"

Rose nodded. "Yes. I asked him if he knew of some place where I might gamble again. I told him that I enjoyed playing cards so much the other night that I was looking for another opportunity to do so. He was very kind, and offered to take me to a card party on Tuesday evening. But he insisted that I wear a domino."

"Wait, I'm confused," Thalia said, bouncing on the bed. "Why do you want to play cards with Lord Kirtland? I thought you were interested in Fungy!"

Rose frowned at Laia. Clearly, she had been filling Thalia's head with romantic nonsense about her and Fungy. "No, Thalia. Lord Kirtland is wealthy and an archeologist. He is much closer to the sort of gentleman I want to marry than Fungy.

"And besides, I did not ask Lord Kirtland to take me to this party just to be with him. I am hoping, if luck is with me, to win all the money we need to pay off our most pressing bills and maybe even more. That way I won't have to worry about marrying quite so quickly," she finished.

Understanding dawned on Thalia. She then clapped her hands in excitement. "You will win all the money we need!"

"Oh yes, Rose, do win lots of money!" Laia said. "Then I can go out and buy more ribbons and Thalia can get a new hat to replace the one she lost in the river, and . . ."

"Laia, please! I've got to win the money first before you spend it all, *and* we've got to pay off our other bills before we mount up any new ones."

"But you will win, Rose, won't you?" Thalia asked, bouncing up and down again.

"I will certainly do my best," she said, leaning back against the pillows on her bed. She tried to control her enthusiasm, while her sisters looked at her happily.

Fungy began to have misgivings about coming to see Lord Halsbury as soon as his lordship started extolling Fungy's admirable qualities.

"You are a very impressive young man, from what I hear of you. Generous—dancing with the wall-flowers, offering fashion advice to those who need it, and apparently, you do all this in such a way as to make everyone not feel the least awkward."

Lord Halsbury offered Fungy a glass of brandy before going on.

"Brummell, y'know, will cut a man down with just the lift of one eyebrow, and let him and all those around know that whatever he is wearing is not good enough. You, on the other hand, simply whisper a word or two into the man's ear—not make a scene of it or embarrass the poor fellow to death. And the advice always takes, because they know you mean well, not just a high-and-mighty arbiter of fashion. Again, very impressive," Halsbury said, hooking his thumb into the watch pocket of his dull brown waistcoat.

Fungy took a large sip of his drink. This was becoming rather embarrassing.

"And, Fotheringay-Phipps—may I call you Fungy? And there's the way you treat the young ladies. Always a kind word. Again if there is the slightest criticism, it is said in such a kind way so that no one could possibly take offense. Why, you must be friends with absolutely everybody!"

"My lord, excuse me for being blunt, but you don't know me. How do you know that I've done any of these things? Don't remember seeing you at many parties."

Lord Halsbury stopped and gave Fungy a wicked smile. "I have my ways."

"Oh?" Now he was really beginning to get worried. What sort of man was Lord Halsbury?

Fungy really didn't know him. All he knew was that Halsbury was very involved in politics, an active member of the House of Lords—and dressed with all the fashion sense of a country squire who rarely came to town. At least his coats were well made to fit his stout figure.

Lord Halsbury got up and pulled the bell cord that was hanging next to the fireplace. A moment later a footman walked into the room.

"James, ask my daughter to step in here a moment, would you?"

The footman bowed and left on his errand.

"I believe you met Harriet at Lady Anson's, did you not?"

"Yes. She spoke with Miss Grace for some time, I believe."

"Yes, that's right. Miss Grace—now there's an interesting girl, aside from the small fact that she has a lot to learn about how to go on in society."

Fungy gave a little laugh, but the picture in his head of Miss Grace was that of an angel calling to him from over the edge of the river. Fungy firmly pushed that image aside as Miss Halsbury came into the room. Fungy stood at her entrance.

She was a quiet girl, not one to push herself forward. Of course, she did not have the beauty to compete with even the prettier girls in society, but she was sweet and gentle. Not nearly as beautiful as Miss Grace, of course.

"Yes, Papa, you wished to see me?" she said, as she closed the door silently behind her.

"Yes, my dear. You remember Mr. Fotheringay-Phipps, er, Fungy?"

"Of course. It is wonderful to see you again, sir." She gave him a small curtsy.

He nodded his head. "The pleasure is mine."

"Fungy wanted to know where I got my information about him and his behavior, my dear."

Miss Halsbury nodded, and gave him a shy little smile. "It is all my fault, I'm afraid."

"There, you see, Fungy. I present to you my social spy. Harriet and her mother go to all of the most fashionable parties so I don't have to. She comes back and tells me about everything and everyone she saw. She seemed to be most impressed with you on the few occasions you've met."

Miss Halsbury's cheeks turned bright pink.

"I had no idea I was being watched," Fungy admitted, rather stunned by this news. It had happened before that a young lady had shown him marked attention, but he had easily discerned her intentions and gently redirected them to another more likely candidate. He had not realized that Miss Halsbury . . .

"I assure you, sir, if it were not for my father, I would not have been so bold," Miss Halsbury said quietly.

"No, no, it was not Harriet's idea to watch you in particular, Fungy. I simply asked her to look out for someone who moved among society easily, and who she thought was intelligent enough to undertake an assignment for me should the need arise."

"And you singled me out, Miss Halsbury?" Fungy was becoming more surprised by the moment.

"Of course, Fungy," Miss Halsbury said, looking as if it was obvious that he was the right man for such work.

"How could you possibly think that I was so intelligent?" he could not help asking.

Miss Halsbury's pink cheeks turned an even deeper shade of that color, but her voice was quite serious when she said, "You may try to hide behind your façade of ennui, but I can see your intelligence in your eyes and in the clever things that you say. You are also very careful in the way you treat people—very thoughtful so as not to hurt anyone's feelings or embarrass them publicly."

"As you see, Fungy, my daughter is an excellent judge of character. I trust her implicitly," Lord Halsbury concurred.

Fungy was stunned. Just from watching him, Miss Halsbury had discerned all this. And she clearly thought him capable and responsible enough to take on whatever assignment her father might need him for.

But his own cousin did not trust him.

Merry had bypassed him in favor of Sin when it came time to choose a godfather for his son. He had thought Fungy too irresponsible and incapable of taking the position seriously. He had even forgotten Fungy's reputation for being one of the brightest students to ever attend Eton.

How had this girl seen these abilities in him, when his own cousin and best friend could not? And how could she see this just by watching him at parties? The thought astounded him.

He had never felt so exposed in all of his life. He might as well be standing here naked in front of this girl. She could see right through him!

With a strong surge of renewed confidence in himself, Fungy turned back to his host. "What sort of, er, assignment is it that you have in mind for me, sir?"

He nodded to Miss Halsbury. "Thank you, Harriet, that will be all."

She gave another quick curtsy and left the room as quietly as she had entered it.

Lord Halsbury got up and plucked a piece of paper off of his desk. Wordlessly, he handed it to Fungy to read. It was addressed to no one, and seemed to be more like an odd list than a letter.

On it were written the names of a number of lesser-known young men, usually younger sons or brothers of wealthy peers, and some older ladies who were not prominent members of society but had such excellent connections that they were welcomed everywhere. Next to each name was an amount of money, anything between five hundred and five thousand pounds.

Three of the names were crossed off with a careful line running through their names. At the top it said, "To watch out for" and at the bottom were the initials P and H.

Fungy looked it over twice and then looked askance at Lord Halsbury.

"It is a list of targets—or victims, if you will—of a gambling scheme that I believe is being very cleverly run from within the *ton*."

Fungy sat up.

"The names crossed off are of people who have recently disappeared from town. Disappeared, I believe, because of their financial straits."

Fungy looked at the note once more and this time read aloud the names that were crossed off. "The Honorable Curtis Flinchley. Yes, I've heard that he had been sent down to rusticate for a while at his father's estate. Lady Amelia Cotsworth." He thought about her for a minute. "I remember meeting her not two weeks ago at Lady Sefton's ball."

"Lost two thousand pounds that night and hasn't been seen since," Lord Halsbury supplied.

"My God!"

"Yes, precisely. This is a nasty business, Fungy, and

we don't know who is masterminding it. But I am determined to find out. As yet, there are no laws against winning another's fortune at a game of cards, but some of us in Parliament are working on that as well."

"Do you know who she lost this money to?" Fungy asked.

"No. If we knew that, it would be easy, wouldn't it? Unfortunately, she lost the money over a long night of play and, it seems, to a number of people. It is quite likely that her vowels are all being bought up by one person, or perhaps all of the people she lost to are involved in the scheme as well. It is difficult to find out for sure. Which is where you come in."

"What is it you need me to do?"

"I want you to find out who is running this scheme and to stop it."

Fungy nearly laughed. "You make it sound so easy."

"Oh no, Fungy, it is not easy at all. The only clue we have is his, or her, initials. But you know everyone who is anyone in the beau monde. If anyone can figure this out, I believe it is you."

Fungy sat back in his chair, taken aback by the level of trust Lord Halsbury had in him. How could he possibly do this?

Then he remembered the quiet confidence Miss Halsbury had shown in him.

He *could* do this. He was intelligent and responsible. He had vowed to change his life to one that was more meaningful and here was the perfect opportunity to do so.

He stood up. "I shall do it."

Lord Halsbury stood as well, and then grasped Fungy's hand. "Excellent! I knew I could count on you."

\* \* \*

Lord Kirtland smiled at Rose, but somehow it didn't make her feel any better. If anything, it made her feel worse. How could she be losing so badly and he still be smiling at her?

It was a smile of encouragement, she told herself. *Why else would he smile at me like that when I am losing?*

And she was sure that her luck would turn any moment now. It had to. She had won so many of the tricks earlier in the evening—this was just a run of bad luck and would end very soon.

Rose took a deep breath, played a card from her hand, and then returned Lord Kirtland's smile from behind her mask. She would not give up hope.

There was no reason to give up yet—aside from the fact that she had already run out of money. Lord Kirtland had already been kind enough to write a vowel on her behalf with the understanding that she would pay him back as soon as she could. And since it was to his good friend, Mr. Aiken, she was sure it would not be a problem. Certainly, by the end of the night, she would have won that money back and more. Much more.

She paused to watch Lord Kirtland play the two of spades. With it, he won the trick.

Rose had to win at least two hundred pounds in order to pay off all of their bills. That shouldn't be too difficult, considering the amounts being wagered. Why, she had already won and lost at least that much. Winning all that she needed was not going to be a problem.

The suit being played was diamonds. Rose didn't have any diamonds. With a little smile, she played a low trump card.

As soon as she had won her two hundred pounds, she would definitely stop, she told herself firmly. She would stop gambling—in fact, she would stop playing cards altogether. All she needed was enough to pay the bills.

Rose swallowed hard as Lord Kirtland took the trick once more, beating her trump card with one of his own. He looked so very pleased with himself, she thought. But this was not going to stop her.

She had to win this money!

Rose took a deep breath to calm herself, and looked over at Lord Kirtland once more. He was now smiling down at his cards. Well, she was glad he was pleased with his hand. She wished she was as pleased with her own.

When he looked up again, he caught her looking at him. Somehow, imperceptibly, his smile changed. His eyes narrowed a bit and one side of his mouth twitched higher than the other. Was it desire that she saw in his eyes? A tremor rushed through her body.

Rose quickly looked back at her cards. Randomly, she put down a card, and then immediately realized that she had made a stupid move. She had played her queen when the king hadn't been played yet.

She wondered if she were falling in love with Lord Kirtland. He certainly made her feel . . . what was the word, unsettled? No, it couldn't be that. Excited, perhaps—just a look from him could send chills up and down her spine.

She had heard that people quite often feel unusual or off-balance when they fall in love. Perhaps that was what was happening to her.

She watched as Mr. Aiken played the king, winning the trick and the rubber. *Oh, dear!*

The cards were gathered, points tallied, and a new hand dealt.

Rose took a deep breath and forced herself to concentrate. She could not afford to make any more mistakes!

# 11

"When your demeanor mimics the name of the game, perhaps it is time to take a break," a gentleman said, as he approached her table.

Rose had just picked up her new hand and taken a first peek at the cards she had been dealt.

She turned toward the gentleman. "Fungy!" All of her muscles, which she hadn't even realized were tense, relaxed.

He looked like a breath of fresh air, all in blue and frothy white. And just like that her own breathing eased. She couldn't help but give him a broad smile. "If you mean to imply that I was looking wistfully at my cards, then, I am afraid, I must admit my guilt."

"Then perhaps it would be best if you sat out this hand and took a stroll about with me?"

He held out his hand for her to take and she grasped onto it as if it were a lifeline. She wondered briefly if he was now saving *her* from drowning, just as he had saved Thalia a few days before.

"That sounds lovely. I am getting a bit of a headache. Some exercise would no doubt do me good."

She turned back to the others at the table. "I do hope you will excuse me . . ."

"Egerton! Rolly Egerton, how are you? Haven't seen you since . . ." a large, red-faced, jovial man interrupted Rose as he strode over to Lord Kirtland.

"Applethwaite!" Lord Kirtland exclaimed, standing up to shake his friend's hand. "Good to see you. Er, it's Kirtland, now. M'father died last year."

"Eh? Oh, sorry about that. So now you've joined high society?"

As the two went into reminiscing, Rose gave a little shrug. "I suppose now *is* a good time to take a break." She placed her hand on Fungy's arm and they walked slowly toward the terrace.

"I am sorry to have interrupted your game, Miss Grace," Fungy said, as he led the way through the room.

"Oh, it is not a problem at all. Like you said, I needed a break."

He nodded. "Looked as if you were having a spot of trouble."

She paused and smiled gratefully up at him. "Always there when I need you, Fungy?"

He turned his eyes on her. The look in them made her feel like someone had just enveloped her in a warm, soft blanket.

"I am always at your service," he said, his voice as soothing as his warm blue eyes.

Rose had trouble tearing her eyes away from his. She could happily drown in those eyes.

As they stepped out onto the terrace, she stopped and took a deep breath of the warm night air. It was filled with sweet scents from the garden, and was more refreshing than anything could have been just then.

With one swift movement, she pushed back her mask from her face and the hood from her head. It felt very good to be free of these physical restrictions.

She then looked at Fungy, who was watching her with a little smile playing on his lips.

"How did you know it was I behind the mask?" she asked.

He touched the Macedonian bracelet on her arm. "This gave you away."

"Oh, yes. You admired it at Lady Anson's soiree. I had forgotten that."

His hand lingered on her arm for a moment, sending heat rushing from that point through her body.

She took a small step away and turned toward the garden. "I must say, it has been quite wonderful being masked. I have been able to do things that a proper young lady would never do."

"Oh? What have you been up to, Miss Grace? Not getting into any more trouble, I hope?" he asked, with a laugh in his voice.

Rose giggled. "Oh no! And how could I, when no one knew it was me? No, I merely walked here, with only Lord Kirtland's escort. And, I hope you will not think me fast, but I have been drinking brandy!"

Fungy raised his eyebrows. "It is uncommon for a young lady to have a taste for brandy."

"I know. My father invited me to drink it with him one evening a few years ago when my mother would not—she thought it improper for a lady to do so. But he does not like to drink alone and there were no other English gentlemen with us on our last expedition, so I drank it with him. Since then when given the opportunity, which isn't often, I assure you, I partake of a little." Rose gave a little giggle.

As she had expected, Fungy was not horrified by this admission. Instead, he smiled. "I see. Must have been lonely when you were on an expedition with your father."

"Oh, no. We always had each other, my sisters and my mother. And we worked quite hard—as hard as my father—cataloguing the things that he found." Rose paused. "That reminds me. I never properly thanked you the other day for saving my sister, Thalia."

Fungy brushed aside her words with a wave of his hand. "Think no more of it. Now tell me, what brings you here to this little gathering? Shouldn't you be dancing at Lady Southwick's ball instead?"

Rose gave him a guilty smile. "Perhaps I should. But when Lord Kirtland told me about this card party, I just had to come and see it for myself," she said, repeating the lie she had practiced just in case anyone asked her this question.

"I do so like new experiences, and to be honest, I do not care for large society parties." Well, that, at least, was the truth, she thought to herself.

"Do not care for balls?" Fungy asked, clearly intrigued.

"I am not used to society. The few parties I have attended I have found to be deathly dull, I'm afraid."

"Ah. But it is all in the attitude, Miss Grace. If you go expecting to be entertained, or enlightened, then yes, they are, as you say, deathly dull. However, if you go with an eye for the absurd, you shall be highly amused, I guarantee it."

She thought about this for a moment and then laughed. "Yes, I do believe that is a good way of thinking about it. I am sure to enjoy myself if I look at things from that perspective. Thank you!"

"Seeing you happy and laughing is all the thanks that I need," he said, half to himself. He then gave a rather embarrassed little laugh. "Perhaps I should return you to your card game."

Reluctantly, she put her mask and hood back on. She loved the freedom being masked afforded her, but she hated how uncomfortable and hot it was.

Fungy took her arm and began to lead her back inside. But just as they had stepped back into the drawing room, Lord Kirtland approached them.

"Ah, I was just coming to see where you were."

"And I was just about to return her to you, my lord," Fungy said.

Despite his words, he seemed reluctant to pass her hand over to Lord Kirtland, and held onto it for perhaps a moment too long.

Rose felt like she was being passed like a card from one player to the next, and she was not entirely sure that she liked it. However, Lord Kirtland was her escort for the evening, and he had been kind enough to bring her here at her insistence, so she supposed she didn't have too much choice in the matter.

The fleeting expression of annoyance on Fungy's face told her that he did not exactly like having to give her up either.

"Have you had enough fresh air, or may I entice you to take a walk with me through the garden? It is a beautiful evening," Lord Kirtland said smoothly, his rich baritone gliding over her like a snake over a patch of sand.

It *was* a beautiful evening and the twinkling lights in the garden had looked very enticing as she and Fungy had stood out on the terrace, so she put aside any feelings of discomfort. Nodding her head in acquiescence, she turned and headed back outside with Lord Kirtland.

They strolled along in silence for a bit, Rose slowly feeling her muscles tense once again. What was it about Lord Kirtland that put her so much on edge, she wondered.

He was very handsome in a rough and rugged way. She supposed all those muscles would come in handy on an archeological dig, if one wanted to do the actual digging oneself.

And it was quite wonderful that Lord Kirtland was an archeologist. That certainly spoke volumes for the way she was feeling—for she was sure that these odd new sensations were caused by the fact that she was attracted to Lord Kirtland. How could she not be when he fit so many of the criteria she was looking for in a husband?

Yes, perhaps that was it. She was just nervous because she knew that he was the perfect man for her.

She smiled up at him as they walked slowly, enjoying the star-strewn night and the garden. Rose willed herself to relax and enjoy the evening.

How wonderful this was, the perfect man for her taking her for a romantic walk through a moonlit garden. She chided herself for feeling anything but pure happiness in the moment. *Just stop thinking, Rose, and enjoy the evening and the company.*

The wonderful smell Rose had noticed from the terrace was caused by rose bushes that lined the walkway. Now, out amongst them, the smell was even more wonderful and intense. The crunching of the gravel beneath their feet as they slowly strolled down the path was the only sound around them, lending a peaceful, calming feeling to their surroundings.

"A more perfect evening, I could not imagine," Rose said, gazing up at the sky.

"Indeed, I feel humbled to be among such beautiful things," Lord Kirtland said.

Rose looked at him and found that he had not been looking at the stars, but at her. She felt her face heat and was grateful for the darkness.

"I hope I did not ruin your game when I left the table," Rose said, deliberately changing the subject.

"No, not at all. Quite all right. My friend, Mr. Applethwaite, took your place for some time." He paused and then said, "I am sorry I did not notice that you had become tired."

"I think I was simply concentrating too hard on the cards. I suppose I'm not used to playing for such a long time."

"No? Do you not play with your sisters?"

"Not whist. We would play casino sometimes, and other children's games. But they are just silliness and fun."

"Yes."

Rose stopped speaking. She had been meaning to make a joke of playing such games, but Lord Kirtland did not seem to be the sort one joked with. He was not at all like Fungy, who was always making light of a situation or a joke about something. Lord Kirtland seemed to be much more serious.

She brushed it aside and focused on enjoying their walk.

As they neared the end of the walkway, Lord Kirtland took her hand from his arm and turned to face her. If he moved even a few inches closer their bodies would be touching, Rose thought with a slight tremor, but she stood her ground and resisted the urge to step away.

"I am so very glad you were able to come with me this evening," he said quietly, putting his hands on her shoulders and pulling her even closer toward him.

Rose swallowed and wondered if he was going to kiss her. "It was very kind of you to ask me."

He bent his head forward, his lips slowly coming closer to hers.

Yes, he was going to kiss her!

His hot breath smelled of the wine he had been drinking.

Rose fought the urge to recoil. She could do this. She was attracted to this man. She wanted to marry him.

At the last moment Rose turned her head so that he kissed her cheek.

What was wrong with her? She was about to receive her first kiss from a handsome man who would make the most perfect husband and solve all of her family's problems. Why could she not kiss him?

He pulled back and chuckled. It was not a very happy sound, however.

"I am sorry, my lord, I, I think . . ."

"Maidenly modesty?" he said, interrupting her.

Rose exhaled with a sigh of relief and then gave a nervous little laugh. "Yes, I suppose that is it. Could, could we go back to the card game? I still owe Mr. Aiken two hundred pounds and I would like to win it back from him."

# 12

The following morning, Rose was awakened by both of her sisters jumping onto her bed.

She moaned and turned over so that she was face down, and covered her head with her quilt.

"Come on, Rose, we have let you sleep long enough. Now you have to tell us how you did last night," Thalia said, shaking her shoulder roughly.

"Yes, and who you met," Laia urged.

"How much money did you win?" Thalia asked eagerly.

"Did Lord Kirtland kiss you?" Laia asked, with the same enthusiasm.

"Go away!" Rose said from under her covers.

"No!" the two girls said in unison.

"Not until you tell us everything," Laia said.

"I think we should go to the park today. You have been putting us off for long enough. Surely you have met enough gentlemen now so that we may go and choose among them," Thalia said eagerly. "Come on, Rose. Do say that we might go today, please?"

"Oh yes, please Rose, we should definitely go to the park this afternoon," Laia added her voice to her younger sister's urging. "Unless there is a gentleman who has invited you out for a drive?"

Rose felt like she was suffocating, so she lowered her covers and turned over. "No, I have not been invited out by anyone." She sighed. "All right, we may go for a ride this afternoon." She paused and then added, "But you both must promise to be on your best behavior, or else I shall never take you to the park during the promenade ever again!"

"Why Rose, whatever makes you think that we would not behave properly?" Thalia asked innocently.

Both Rose and Laia gave her such a look that very soon all three girls were giggling away.

"But you still haven't told us about last night," Laia complained.

"Yes. How much money did you win?" Thalia asked again.

Rose sat up, propping her pillows behind her. She then clasped her hands in her lap and stared down at them unable to look her sisters in the eye. "I didn't win any. In fact, I lost all that I had and more, I'm afraid."

"And more? How could you lose more than you had?" Laia gasped.

"Lord Kirtland had to pay my debt to his friend, Mr. Aiken, and accepted a vowel from me—a promissory note saying that I would pay him one hundred pounds."

"One hundred . . ." Laia started to scream.

Rose immediately clasped her hand over her sister's mouth. "Shhh! If Aunt Farmington or Papa were to hear you . . ."

"Oh, Rose! Where are you going to get so much money?" Thalia asked in a whisper, as soon as Rose had removed her hand.

"I don't know. I suppose I'll just have to win it

back. I had lost two hundred to him, but then won back half of it."

"Oh, well that is good, I suppose," Laia said, a little uncertainly.

"Was Fungy there?" Thalia asked.

"Yes, he was. He took me out for a breath of air on the terrace," Rose admitted.

Laia squeaked. "He did? How romantic!"

Rose thought about that for a moment and then said, "No, it really wasn't very romantic. It was just very pleasant. He is a very kind man. And very funny. He always makes me laugh."

"And makes you feel good? Does he give you tingles?" Laia asked.

"Laia! You should not know of such things!" Rose scolded her sister.

"Well, but does he?" she persisted.

Rose smiled. "He does make me feel good. But then Lord Kirtland took me for a walk through the garden and that was *very* romantic."

"Did he kiss you?" Laia asked, scrunching up closer.

"No! He is a gentleman. He would not do that unless he had asked me to marry him first," Rose lied. She was not about to admit to her sisters that she had backed out of her first kiss.

"I don't know that I like Lord Kirtland," Thalia said thoughtfully.

"You've never met him!" Rose objected.

"Well, no, but from all I've heard . . ."

"He is a very nice man, and very romantic," Rose said, defending him.

"Hmph," her sister said, unconvinced. Rose knew that romance held very little weight with Thalia, as opposed to Laia, who was much more like herself and had a very romantic nature. But Thalia was too young for that yet.

"He is an archeologist like Papa. And quite wealthy,"

Rose said. "Do you know what he said when I was losing? He laughed, and said that it was just a game! As if there was no money involved!"

"My goodness, he *must* have a lot of money to think so little of it," Thalia cooed.

"Yes, my thoughts exactly."

"So you think he is the one you should marry, Rose?" Laia asked, a little sadly.

Rose nodded her head. "I am thinking very seriously of it. He is as close to my ideal husband as I'm going to find at such short notice."

Her sisters sat back quietly thinking about this, as did Rose.

She was certain that this was the right answer, and if he didn't give her tingles like Fungy did, well, she supposed that that was all right. Perhaps she would feel that way after they had known each other a little longer. She was sure her nervousness and chills that she felt when she was with him were just a prelude to a lot of tingles.

The rhythmic thwacking sound of the punching ball lulled Fungy into a mindless haze. Once he had got into the rhythm of the punching bag, he no longer needed to think about what he was doing. The physical release of the constant punching was very relaxing. Right. Left. Right. Left. Right, right. Left, left.

As his mind started to drift off among the quiet hubbub of Gentleman Jackson's Boxing Salon, Fungy noticed that this was not as relaxing as it normally was.

Perhaps it was him. He had had a most difficult time of it recently. In a very short period of time his entire life had been turned upside down.

But what still disturbed him the most was . . .

"Good morning, Fungy."

. . . Merry.

Fungy stopped hitting the punching bag just in front of his face. Turning he saw his cousin, with his good friend, Sin, Lord Reath, strolling past him on their way to the two punching bags next to his.

"Doing well," Sin said, unbuttoning his waistcoat and taking it and his coat off together.

"He always has excellent form," Merry commented, taking off his own coat.

"Good morning, gentlemen," Fungy said coldly.

Merry paused to look at him before taking off his waistcoat. He then placed it on the back of the chair on top of his coat. "Haven't seen you around recently. Is everything all right?"

"Fine. Just fine, thank you. Yourself?" Fungy asked, trying to keep his voice neutral.

"I've been well."

"Teresa and the baby?"

"They are doing very well. Teresa finally settled on a nursemaid, so we have all been getting more sleep."

"Glad to hear that." Fungy turned back to the ball, but it no longer looked so interesting.

He took a step toward his cousin. "Care to spar with me, Merry?"

Both men turned in surprise to him.

"*You* want to fight, Fungy?" Sin asked.

"Yes, is there a problem with that?"

"No, it is just that I don't believe I've ever seen you actually sparring with anyone before. You usually just work the bag."

"Yes, but today I am in the mood for something different. What do you say, Cousin?"

Merry gave him a little bow. "I would be happy to." He then gave Fungy a teasing smile. "Do you really think you stand a chance? I'm a bit heavier than you are."

"No matter. I can take you on," Fungy responded quickly.

Merry laughed. "That's what you always said when we were little and I would still always beat you."

Fungy found nothing amusing in this. He just flexed his hands. "And I thought you had completely forgotten our youth."

With that parting shot, he stepped into the ring in the center of the room, and waited for his cousin to join him.

"What was that supposed to mean?" Merry asked, following him.

"Only that you and Sin both seemed to have conveniently forgotten both our youth and me." And with that he hit Merry hard across his jaw.

Merry wasn't prepared, and he dropped to the floor like a stone.

Sin jumped into the ring to help him up. "I say, Fungy, that was not fair."

"Why not? He should have been ready." Fungy moved from foot to foot. "Come on, Merry. What's your problem? Have you forgotten your boast of just a few minutes ago as well?"

Merry shrugged Sin off of him and put up his fists, now ready for an earnest fight. "I don't know what your problem is, Fungy, but if you want a fight, I'm ready."

Merry mostly defended himself, as Fungy held nothing back. In a surge of flying fists, he released all of his anger and hurt on his cousin.

How could Merry think him irresponsible? Hook right. How could he not trust him? Uppercut left. Why could an utter stranger see through his façade while his own best friend and cousin whom he had grown up with could not see past it? He punched him a doubler with a quick left-right combination, coming down hard with his right.

How was it that Merry had so conveniently forgotten how responsible Fungy had been when they were together in school? All he saw now was Fungy's precise dressing and his outward demeanor of ennui. Merry had forgotten who St. John Fotheringay-Phipps really was—and that hurt more than anything else.

Fungy landed another well-placed right hook to his cousin's jaw and Merry went down, but Fungy wasn't finished. He dropped to one knee and continued pummeling his cousin, giving free rein to all of his latent anger. He was past caring or even thinking about what he was actually doing. All he cared about now was beating out all of his fury on the one who had caused it.

A strong hand grabbed his arm as he was about to land another blow to Merry's jaw, and pulled him back and to his feet.

He spun around, ready to attack whoever it was who had pulled him away, but found his nose within inches of Gentleman Jackson himself. The man, although shorter than Fungy, was a good deal larger and immeasurably stronger.

"I think that is enough, sir," he said quietly, but firmly.

Fungy backed down.

"My God, did you see that? He floored Merrick like he was nothing." He heard one onlooker say to another.

"Got a bit out of control there, didn't he?" the second gentleman said.

"Not quite a fair mill. Merrick didn't stand a chance under that onslaught," said another.

Fungy took a deep breath then turned around and extended his hand down to his cousin.

He was still breathing hard, but the pounding in Fungy's head was beginning to subside. Never before had he ever wanted to hurt anyone as much as he had wanted to hurt Merry. And as he helped his cousin to stand up, he prayed that he never would again.

Merry's face was already beginning to turn black and

blue. Sin quickly handed him a handkerchief to stem the trickle of blood that was dripping from his nose.

Fungy walked from the ring and began to dress. He was carefully tying his neckcloth in front of a mirror when Merry came up behind him, still buttoning his waistcoat, and touched him on the shoulder.

"Shall we dine at Whites?"

"Happy to."

For the first time in a while, Fungy felt quite light-hearted, and much more like his old cheery self.

As he walked out with Sin and his cousin, who was smiling and joking even through his slightly battered face, Fungy felt a pang of contrition. He wondered for a moment whether he ought to thank his cousin for understanding him so well, and for letting him take out his frustrations on him.

But he kept his own counsel, knowing that the thanks would be more uncomfortable for his cousin than the injuries he had just sustained.

# 13

"Who is that, Rose? That is certainly the most handsome horse I have seen yet," Thalia said, looking ahead to their left, where a gentleman riding a black gelding was coming toward them.

"I believe that is Lord Hawksmore. He is a duke. I am certain that he would not even look my way."

"Oh."

"What about the gentleman over there, driving that high-perch phaeton with the bright yellow wheels? He is very handsome," Laia said, straining her neck to get a better view.

"Laia, sit properly. You look like you are about to fall off your horse," Rose reprimanded her sister.

Laia shifted herself back into her proper position and frowned at Rose. "Well, I don't see how we can see anybody, with this line moving so very slowly," she complained.

"But that is the way it is in the park at this time of day. If you want to see anyone, you must be patient."

"Oh, look!"

"What Thalia, is it another horse with very fine points?" Laia asked, sounding extremely bored.

Thalia whipped her head around and looked like

she was about to stick her tongue out at her sister. She refrained, however, and merely said in her haughtiest voice, "It is a very handsome *man*, if you want to know."

"Where?" Laia was instantly very interested, and stretched her neck out once more to see where her sister had been looking.

"Ha! You are only interested in the men."

"Well, that is what we are here for after all—not to look at horses! Rose doesn't want to marry a horse."

"All right, that is enough," Rose said, with as much authority as she could muster without bursting out laughing at her sisters' ridiculous bickering.

They had been riding around the park for nearly thirty minutes. Rose figured that her sisters must be getting tired, which would explain their shortened tempers.

She knew that she, too, was becoming rather downcast. Looking at so many gentlemen was not going to help her to find a rich husband. And she was not entirely sure that this was the best use of her time.

What she needed was another opportunity to play cards. It was the only way out of her current dilemma.

She *had* to win back the vowel she had written to Lord Kirtland. And then, if she could, win more to pay off their bills. Only then would everything be all right. But just now, it was her debt to Lord Kirtland that was worrying her the most.

Of course, if she married Lord Kirtland the problem would be solved, a little voice in the back of her head reminded her.

Yes, but . . . and he did try to kiss her last night.

"It is not fair! Thalia is much taller than I am, she can see more," Laia complained, abruptly bringing Rose's mind back to the present.

Rose ignored her and asked, "Thalia, who did you

see that you were exclaiming over just a moment ago?"

"It is Fungy, Rose, over there." This time she pointed with her finger, despite Rose having told her not to do so numerous times.

Rose did not reprimand her sister again, but merely turned to see that it was indeed Fungy. He was driving a beautiful bright red phaeton, pulled by a very fine looking black horse.

Not to be outdone by his equipage, Fungy himself was wearing a deep green double-breasted coat, which showed off his broad shoulders and narrow waist. If Rose had not already known that his shoulders and arms were muscular, from having seen him without his coat on the day he saved Thalia from the river, his clothing today would have left no doubt to it at all.

"Oh, my." Laia sighed.

Rose echoed the sentiment, but had the presence of mind not to say so out loud.

Then he leaned back, laughing at something, and Rose caught a glimpse of his companion. She felt as if the breath had been taken from her body.

Fungy had invited Miss Halsbury out for a drive!

"Who is that young lady with whom he is driving? Do you know her, Rose?" Thalia asked.

Rose had trouble answering her at first, but then she reprimanded herself for her petty jealousy and said, "Harriet Halsbury. She is a very nice girl. I met her at Lady Anson's soiree."

There was no reason why she should be jealous of Miss Halsbury, Rose told herself sternly. She was not interested in Fungy. She was going to marry Lord Kirtland.

That thought stopped her for a moment. Had she actually made up her mind to marry him? Mentally, she shrugged. She supposed she had.

She then nodded to herself. Yes, she was absolutely

right. She *was* going to marry Lord Kirtland. Fungy was just a very kind, and handsome, friend—nothing more.

In fact, she told herself, she was very happy he was out with Miss Halsbury. She liked Miss Halsbury.

"What is he doing driving with her?" Laia asked, peevishly.

"Why should he not?" Rose asked.

"Because he should be out driving with you," Thalia answered for her older sister.

"Yes," Laia concurred.

"No. He should be out driving with whomever he wants. And clearly, he wants to be with Miss Halsbury." Rose spurred her horse toward Fungy's phaeton. "Come, let's say hello."

Fungy reined in his horse as soon as he saw Rose and her sisters approaching.

"How do you do, Miss Grace, Miss Thalia, Miss Laia," he said, nodding his head to each of the sisters in turn.

"How do you do, Fungy? How nice to see you, Miss Halsbury. It is a lovely day for a ride, is it not?" Rose said, brightly.

"Fungy, it is good to see you again," Laia said, warmly.

"How do you do?" Thalia added, nodding to both Fungy and Miss Halsbury.

Rose introduced her younger sisters to Miss Halsbury, who smiled sweetly at them, but said nothing.

"I do hope you haven't had the urge to go swimming again, Miss Thalia?" Fungy asked, smiling at her.

Thalia laughed. "No, sir. I think I shall follow your advice and wait until we go out into the country to do that again."

"Do you enjoy swimming, Miss Thalia?" Miss Halsbury asked.

"Yes, I do, but that is not what Fungy is referring to," she said, giggling.

"Unfortunately, Thalia had a little mishap at the docks the other day and ended up in the river. Fungy was kind enough to help her out again," Rose explained briefly.

"What do you mean, help her out again? You make it sound so tame, Rose," Laia objected. "She fell into the water, Miss Halsbury, and her dress caught on something so that she could not swim back to dock by herself. Fungy was incredibly brave and dove in after her. He nearly drowned in the process of saving her!"

"Oh, my!"

"Miss Laia's version does make it sound much more exciting, but it was nothing, really," Fungy said, dismissively. He then turned to Thalia. "Glad you suffered no ill effects, Miss Thalia."

"None at all. Did you? You seemed to be a little upset by the whole thing," Thalia said, looking at Fungy with concern.

"Thalia!" Rose protested her sister's blunt honesty.

"It is all right, Miss Grace," Fungy said. "I was, indeed, a little upset by it. Diving into the river is not very pleasant, nor is nearly drowning. However, Miss Thalia, thanks to your eldest sister, I am perfectly well to tell the tale."

Laia and Thalia looked to Rose in surprise, but she had no idea what he was talking about. She was no less shocked by this pronouncement than her sisters seemed to be. "Me? Whatever did I do, sir?"

Fungy looked at her with disconcerting warmth. "Why, you called out to me, Miss Grace. It was your sweet voice that called me back from the watery depths."

"Oh." Rose did not know what to say, but for some reason she found herself with a great desire to reach out and take Fungy's hand, or to touch him in some way. Their eyes locked for just the briefest moment, but in that short space of time she knew that he was feeling the same way.

The tingles that she had been thinking about just that morning went rushing through her body and she forgot that anyone else was nearby as she lost herself in his deep blue smiling eyes.

Her horse shifted under her and she was brought back to reality with a jolt.

"You were so long under the water," she stammered by way of explanation, feeling the stares of her sisters as well as Miss Halsbury. And she knew that she must be blushing furiously.

"Ah, well, now my little secret is out, I suppose." Fungy's cheeks too turned slightly pink. Rose guessed that he had not meant to reveal this personal moment to anyone.

There was an awkward silence, and then a voice called from behind Fungy's phaeton. "I say, Fungy, are you going to begin moving again or do I have to try and go around you?"

A look of relief swept over his face as Fungy turned around and waved at the gentleman behind him. "You will have to excuse us, Miss Grace . . ." he began.

"Of course," she said, and turned her horse quickly so that she and her sisters could reenter the flow of traffic going the other way. "Good-bye. It was very nice seeing you again, Miss Halsbury. You will have to stop by and pay us a visit," she said, just before riding away.

It wasn't that she was anxious to get away from Fungy, she thought as she kicked her horse into a trot, it was simply too embarrassing a situation, and to have had to endure that with her sisters watching . . . well, she just hoped that they wouldn't question her about it later. And it had nothing to do with her feelings for Fungy because he was simply a friend, she reminded herself firmly, despite the tingles.

* * *

Fungy saw Miss Halsbury looking shrewdly at him as they continued on their drive through the park.

He was sure that the ever-perceptive Miss Halsbury knew exactly what was on his mind—*why in heaven's name had he told them all that Miss Grace had saved him from drowning?*

The problem was that he had absolutely no idea why he had done that. He had not wanted to make Miss Grace feel awkward—which she had, naturally. He had not wanted Miss Halsbury to feel as if he wanted to be with Miss Grace rather than her—which just might be the truth, but that was not the point.

He should not have revealed himself in this way, that was the point. It was very unlike him to do so. And the look which they shared—it was simply not something one did in public!

"Miss Halsbury, you must excuse my lapse. Cannot imagine what caused me to even mention that Miss Grace had called out to me."

"It is quite obvious why, Fungy," Miss Halsbury said quietly.

"Indeed, no. Not at all what you think. Why, I have rarely enjoyed an afternoon spent in a young lady's company as much as I have enjoyed our time together today."

"That is very kind of you to say . . ."

"Not just saying it, Miss Halsbury, I truly mean it. You are as delightful as a summer's day, as sweet as the most delicious confection—although thankfully, not sticky at all."

Miss Halsbury laughed. "You shall soon have me blushing, Fungy."

"Nothing wrong with a little flirtation, Miss Halsbury. Rather expected, I would think."

"Yes, I suppose so, but entirely unnecessary, I assure

you." She turned her attention back to the people all around them, with a smile on her lips. Fungy felt as if he had had a narrow escape.

He stole a glance over at Harriet Halsbury. She was a very pleasant young lady, but definitely not his type. He sensed that she knew that, and therefore did not expect him to woo her. It was a good thing—she deserved better than him.

Miss Grace, on the other hand, was surely the road to his destruction. She caused him to lose control over his carefully constructed persona, and to say such ridiculous things as he had done today. She encouraged him to do more and to be more. She had him quoting De La Rochefoucauld, reading Greek, wanting to save her and her sisters from the awkward situations they got themselves into, and making him think of things he had not thought of since before his first love, Georgiana, left him and took his heart with her.

No, it would be best if he stayed as far away from Miss Rose Grace as possible.

—

# 14

Rose was more than pleased by Lord Kirtland's invitation to visit the British Museum. The card was waiting for her, together with a beautiful bouquet of flowers, when she and her sisters arrived home from their ride in the park.

It confirmed to Rose that she was indeed making the right choice in deciding to marry Lord Kirtland.

He would never make awkward admissions regarding her in public. And he never sent tingles through her body with just a look from his warm and laughing eyes.

He was, however, as romantic and thoughtful as she had always dreamed a gentleman should be, and she could hardly wait for the following day when they would meet.

What was less pleasant, but also awaiting her on the side table with Lord Kirtland's invitation, was another bill from the modiste and a simple note reminding Lord Pemberton-Howe that payment was expected.

Although addressed to her father, it was clear that he had read it, and left it for her—a not so subtle hint that it was up to her to do something to ensure that the bill could be paid.

Rose was tempted to crumple up the note and the bill and throw them both into the fire. But she could not do that—not only was there no fire, but she knew that the woman had to be paid.

She turned back to the invitation from Lord Kirtland, knowing that he was her only hope.


"How wonderful this is, my lord," Rose said, trying hard to contain her enthusiasm.

"I am so glad you think so, Miss Grace," Lord Kirtland said as he slowly led Rose through the first room of exhibits at the British Museum.

"I have been wanting to come to see the museum ever since we first arrived in London. Unfortunately, with my social obligations and settling my family here, I just have not had the chance. I can't tell you how much I appreciate your thoughtful offer to bring me here today."

"It is entirely my pleasure."

"Oh, look!" Rose moved forward eagerly to see a mummy in its coffin.

Lord Kirtland held back a little, but Rose gestured for him to join her at the mummy's side.

"Isn't it fascinating? Just look at how well preserved he is. It just astounds me how the ancient Egyptians learned to embalm a body so that it could last for centuries."

"Indeed."

"My father worked closely with Belzoni in Egypt for a number of years, excavating a tomb. The Egyptians were extraordinarily thoughtful when putting together tombs for the dead. Everything a person might need in order to live comfortably in the afterlife was provided."

"Really? Er, yes, I have heard of such things, of course."

"They included mummified meat, as well as dried fruits, and numerous jars and bowls and even money. Absolutely everything that one needed in order to live."

"They found food with the bodies?" a young man standing next to Rose asked.

"Oh yes. It was believed . . ."

"Please, my lord, I cannot stand here looking at that thing. Oh, I am feeling decidedly unwell," the young lady on the gentleman's arm complained, while putting a limp hand to her forehead. Indeed, she was looking quite pale.

The man was clearly surprised to see his companion looking this way, and immediately escorted her away to sit down on one of the numerous benches in the hall.

Rose turned back to Lord Kirtland and noticed that he too was looking rather pale.

"Perhaps we should move on," she suggested.

"Yes, I think that would be an excellent idea," he said with obvious relief.

He led the way toward a display of jewelry that had also been found in the tomb. "Now here is something quite fascinating. You ladies always like looking at jewelry, do you not?"

Rose was, in fact, not so interested in the jewelry, but she gave him a little smile and tried to live up to his expectation.

"My word, that must cost thousands of pounds, don't you think, Miss Grace?" Lord Kirtland asked, examining the large gold necklet that had adorned the mummy.

"I really couldn't say." Rose looked back at the young lady and gentleman, who were now sitting and holding hands on a bench on the other side of the

room. The young lady seemed to be completely recovered and was giggling over something the gentleman was saying.

She caught Rose's eye and then began laughing in
earnest, so much so that she had to cover her mouth
with her hand.

Rose could not imagine what she had found to be
so amusing in a museum, but turned back to Lord Kirtland, who was now examining a wide gold armband.

"Look at the craftsmanship on this piece, Miss
Grace," he said, completely absorbed in his study of
the armband.

"Yes, it is quite pretty. Shall we move on?" Rose
wanted to see the coffin of the other mummy. "I
have heard that the inscriptions on the other coffin
are believed to have something to do with the god
Osiris."

"Ah, yes. I believe I may have heard something to
the effect," Lord Kirtland said, slowly walking away
from the jewelry. His steps slowed even more as they
approached the second mummy and its coffin.

Rose paused. Looking up into Lord Kirtland's face,
she noticed him beginning to pale once again. "If you
would prefer, we could just look at the lid which
seems to be over there." Rose pointed away from the
mummy, toward where the lid to the coffin was placed
apart for inspection.

"Yes, yes. A much better idea. I, er, wouldn't want
you to feel unwell like that other young lady."

"How very thoughtful of you, my lord," Rose said
wryly, while trying hard not to smile at Lord Kirtland's
obvious cover-up of his own discomfort.

"I do so enjoy looking at the hieroglyphs and imag-
ining what they might mean," she said, looking over
the coffin lid.

"Yes, and look at all of the gold! Why, it is amazing,"
Lord Kirtland said, taking a step back to admire the

upper half of the lid, which was entirely covered with the precious metal.

"She looks rather lifelike, doesn't she?" Rose said, looking at the face painted at the top.

"Yes. Disturbingly so." Lord Kirtland led Rose away, saying, "I don't believe there was any jewelry associated with this mummy."

"No." Rose was not nearly as disappointed in this as Lord Kirtland seemed to be.

As they moved away from the pieces that interested Rose the most, she began to notice that many of the benches in the museum were occupied by young couples. And what amazed her even more was that they seemed to be completely oblivious to their magnificent surroundings.

Although there were a few older couples and groups of gentlemen wandering around looking at the exhibits, the museum also seemed to be just another place where members of the beau monde went to see and be seen. Men and women wandered the rooms of the museum, hardly looking at the magnificent artifacts surrounding them, but instead seeming to be more interested in the other patrons. There were even groups of people just standing around talking, and when Rose passed by one of them, she was certain that it was not the museum or exhibits that was the main topic of discussion. This was especially true in the room that held the now famous Elgin marbles.

Just seeing these fantastic sculptures outside of their natural habitat made Rose's blood boil with anger. But she held her tongue. She did not wish to engage in another debate over it with Lord Kirtland, who was clearly a strong proponent of the other side of this argument. But, now, considering that Rose had decided to marry the gentleman, she supposed she ought not to argue with him—even an argument of academic nature could be taken quite personally.

Instead, she commented on all that she saw around her. "It just amazes me that so many people can come here and not even look at the exhibits," she said quietly, so that only Lord Kirtland would hear her.

"Well, it is a social outing to come to the museum," he said. "And most young ladies do not have the same interest in these artifacts as you do."

"Yes, it is a shame, but I see that you are quite correct."

"A shame, Miss Grace? Why do you think so?"

"Why? Well, because most of the girls of the *ton* do not seem to have been taught how to think beyond fashion and flirtation, my lord. There is so much more to life than society."

Lord Kirtland stopped and smiled down at Rose. "This is what makes you so very unique, Miss Grace."

Rose felt her face heat. In that moment, she could imagine many happy years with Lord Kirtland, rummaging through the dirt and exciting finds of an archeological expedition. What a happy life that would be!

Nothing at all like the mindless meaninglessness of English society. Fungy, despite his kindness, was merely a reflection of that society. He was just as taken up by vagaries of fashion as the silly women who sat about all day gossiping over their tea.

How happy Rose was to have found Lord Kirtland. He was a true intellectual—and even better, a wealthy one!

# 15

Fungy resisted the urge to take out his handkerchief and press it to his nose. The combined smell of liquor, smoke, and nervous men was almost too much. But he had to be here. He really did not have any choice in the matter. He supposed that this is what it smelled like to work.

This was the smell of responsibility.

It wasn't that Fungy had never been in a gambling hell before—it was simply that he preferred the overly perfumed smell of a ballroom to this. He also had no great love of gambling, aside from the occasional rubber of whist with his friends. But Lord Halsbury was expecting a preliminary report tomorrow morning on his investigation into this gambling scheme—and so far, Fungy had nothing to tell him.

Hopefully something would turn up tonight in this foul-smelling place.

The problem was that he had absolutely no idea what he was doing. There was nothing much one could discern from just watching others play. And yet, what else could he do?

Fungy sighed, and once again cast his keen eyes over the proceedings. Well, one thing was for certain.

Gentlemen who came to gaming hells did not take as much time as they should over their toilettes. He counted at least six badly tied neckcloths. And there were at least seven or eight gentlemen who had worn waistcoats that did not match either their coats or their pantaloons. There were even a few gentlemen in breeches!

Fungy forced himself to stop looking at the gentlemen's clothing and concentrate instead on the games they were playing. Who was losing to whom? There had to be some telltale sign that would point toward someone who was cheating.

He moved slowly around the room of the gambling hell, where the sound of coins clinking together intermingled with the men's voices.

Pausing for a few minutes at one table to watch a card game, he caught the eye of a woman of evidently dubious morals. She rubbed herself suggestively against the back of the man sitting directly in front of her, but her eyes were on Fungy.

He quickly broke his gaze and moved on, avoiding that table.

Thinking back to the letter Lord Halsbury had shown him, he tried to remember some of the names listed there. Were any of those people here tonight?

He caught sight of Jack Abbey, the Duke of Hawksmore's cousin and heir. His name had been there. And sitting at another table not far away was George Cole, Lord Chester's youngest son. His name had been there too. There was no way that Fungy could watch both men. Randomly, he picked Abbey.

Abbey was playing with Pip Haston, his cousin Hawksmore, and Charles Bradmore. All three men were well known to Fungy, and he could not imagine any one of them leading a gambling ring. But then he remembered the initials at the bottom of the letter—P.H.

Hawksmore? No, his given name was Dominic.
Pip Haston?

Fungy began to watch the game more intently,
moving around to stand near enough to Haston so
that he could see if he was doing anything unusual.

Haston was a dandy of the first order. A true imi-
tator of Fungy's style, who then took it up one notch.
There was something ingenuous about the young
man, or so Fungy had always thought. But perhaps
there was more there than met the eye.

"I say, see Lady Margaret last night at the Peyton's?
Smashing gown she had on, what?" Haston said, as he
placed a card on the table.

Bradmore laughed. "Barely had on, don't you
mean? Her dresses are getting more daring by the
week—soon there will be no top to them at all!"

"Think she's getting a little desperate for a husband?" Hawksmore laughed, as he played his card. For
a duke, he was remarkably easygoing. He would be a
stunning catch for a girl like Lady Margaret, or in fact
for any young lady—not bad to look at and a remarkably nice fellow.

"I'd be interested if her father were a little less ex-
acting in wanting a title," Pip said in a good-natured
way as he lost the trick.

"Would you be interested in her, Jack?" Hawksmore
asked, as he placed the first card down on the table
for the next trick.

"Who me? With Lady Margaret? You must be kid-
ding, cuz. She's sweet, but nothing in the attic."
Abbey played a trump. But he was just the sort he
could see with Lady Margaret, Fungy thought to himself. Such an upright, almost staid young man paired
with her flamboyance would no doubt cause some interesting sparks.

"Thought you liked that sort," Bradmore said as he
waited his turn.

Haston also put down a trump, but it was lower than Abbey's. Fungy didn't quite see the point of that. It was either all he had, or he was deliberately trying to lose.

"No, thank you. I think I shall leave her for some other lucky fellow. Not in the petticoat line just yet, anyway." Abbey began to pick up the cards on the table one by one, having won the trick.

"Oh, damn! Didn't mean to put down that card," Haston exclaimed as he watched Abbey pick up his card.

The men laughed. No, there could be no possibility that Pip Haston was the man Fungy was looking for.

"Fungy! What are you doing here?" Merry said, slapping him on the back. The men at the table all turned to look up at him.

"Fungy, didn't see you standing there. Been there long?" Haston asked.

"Oh, er, not long. Do better to watch what you put down, Haston. Getting yourself distracted with your own chatter."

Fungy laughed, and the other men at the table laughed as well.

"That's why we like to play with him," Hawksmore said.

Haston had the grace to blush, but hid it by taking a long sip from his brandy. "Not very good at this," he said sheepishly when he had put down his glass.

"So what are you doing here?" Merry said to Fungy again. With some relief, Fungy noticed that his handsome, friendly face had healed completely from the boxing match.

"Don't believe I've ever seen you in a gaming hell before," Sin, who was standing just behind Merry, added.

"Oh, just thought I'd stop in and watch a bit before heading off to Lady Roseberry's ball." Fungy shrugged.

He then pulled out his watch and took a look at the time.

It was nearly ten-thirty. Not too late to drop in on the ball. He was a little worried that whoever it was he was looking for wouldn't be here for another few hours. But now that he had committed himself, he had no choice but to abandon his search for the evening.

"Don't mean to scare you off," Merry said.

"Yes, why don't you stay and play a rubber with us?" Sin asked. After having given up playing cards for many years, he had recently begun to play again, but now with much more control than in his salad days. He had had the unfortunate experience of accidentally bankrupting a family when he had won their estate in a game of cards. Of course, it had all worked out for the best—he was now very happily married to the granddaughter of the fellow from whom he won the estate.

"Not sure I have the time. Should really get over to Lady Roseberry's. Hadn't meant to stay this long as it is," Fungy said. He then took himself off before anyone could say anything.

*Whew! That was close.* He would have to watch himself more closely. He could not risk anyone—not even his closest friends—finding out what he was doing. He had promised Lord Halsbury that he would disclose his occupation to no one.

Of course, now he would have no information to disclose to Lord Halsbury either.

Fungy hailed a hackney and directed the driver to the Roseberry's.

Well, at least he had eliminated one person with the initials P.H. Were there any others that he knew of? Fungy ran through a mental list of all the people he knew, searching for someone with those particular initials.

The only one he could come up with was Lord

Pemberton-Howe, Miss Grace's father. But that was impossible. He wasn't the gambling sort, though Fungy supposed he was intelligent enough to organize such a thing.

Fungy wondered what his finances were like. He had to have spent a great deal of money on his expeditions. Could it be that he was desperate for cash—so desperate that he would hire people to cheat at cards for him?

No. Fungy just could not see Lord Pemberton-Howe in that role. Besides, Miss Grace and her sisters were all very well dressed. If he were in financial straits, it was unlikely that he would spend the money necessary to dress his daughters so well.

That meant that there had to be somebody else.

Lord Kirtland bowed to Rose as the orchestra played the final notes of the country dance. Rose was certain that there would soon be talk, for that was the third time she and Lord Kirtland had danced together that evening.

She tried to hide the silly smile that had plagued her all through the dance.

Lord Kirtland was certain to ask her to marry him. There was absolutely no doubt about that in her mind. Not now. Not after asking her to dance three times.

She had been happy when he'd asked her to dance a second time. That meant that he truly was interested in her. But a *third* time? Well, there could be no clearer indication of his intentions.

"I do hope you will excuse me, Miss Grace," Lord Kirtland said, breaking into her thoughts as he returned her to her aunt.

Rose nodded, flashing him a bright smile, and

then watched him make his way directly for the card room.

She sighed happily. Despite her sisters' protestations that Fungy was the man for her, Rose was still firmly of the belief that she could not have found a more perfect gentleman to marry than Lord Kirtland.

She wondered how he was going to propose. Would he visit her and then get down on one knee in front of her? Would he take her for a moonlit walk through a lovely rose garden? Or perhaps he would take her for another romantic tour of the British Museum? Only this time, would it be her sitting on a bench oblivious to her surroundings as Lord Kirtland whispered words of love in her ear and asked her to spend the rest of her life with him?

"Good evening, Miss Grace. You look lovely in that particular shade of pink. Should definitely wear such colors more often." She heard Fungy's voice, and looked up to find him smiling warmly down at her.

"Oh, Fungy! How do you do?" Rose laughed at having been caught in her fantasies. "I am afraid I was woolgathering and didn't see you approach."

He was looking quite magnificent in a coat of dark green superfine and cream-colored pantaloons. His neckcloth flowed down into his waistcoat in what Rose thought must be what was called a waterfall, and his waistcoat was cream, shot with gold with a lovely green floral pattern. Complete, as ever, to a shade.

"Seemed to be thinking of something very pleasant, by the smile you had on your face."

Rose felt her face heat. "Did I? Oh, how very silly of me!"

"Almost hate to tear you away from your happy thoughts, but wondered if you might grant me the next dance?"

"I would be honored, sir," she said quickly, to cover up her embarrassment.

But then, to Rose's dismay, the orchestra began playing the introductory chords for a waltz. Dancing such an intimate dance with Fungy, just after her three dances with Lord Kirtland, somehow seemed . . . awkward, almost like a betrayal. But she did not have a good excuse to sit it out either, as she had recently been granted permission to dance it by the lady patronesses of Almack's. She had no choice but to take Fungy's hand and then allow him to place his other hand on the small of her back.

Luscious tingles shot through her body at his touch.

How was it that she always got these odd sensations whenever Fungy touched her, and yet completely different feelings when it was Lord Kirtland?

She looked up into Fungy's eyes. He looked so happy to be with her! The now-familiar feeling of being blanketed and warm came over her. What was it about this man that made her feel so safe and cared for when she was with him?

It was nearly the opposite feeling that Lord Kirtland inspired. And yet she was going to marry him. But he had so many other wonderful qualities, she reminded herself.

He just never made her feel like this.

Fungy's lips were turned up in a small smile, and his eyes held hers in what felt like a loving embrace. He looked like he could happily stay this way for the rest of his life.

Oh yes, and so could she.

But she should not, her mind screamed to her. She was going to marry Lord Kirtland. She should not be feeling this way.

Yet, the heat of Fungy's body was so close to hers—warming her, enveloping her, protecting her. She felt so good, so feminine and happy.

Rose tried to fight the feelings. Tried to turn her eyes away from his. But it was impossible.

She was lost. Lost in his eyes. Lost in his presence. Lost in everything that was him. And slowly, she let her thoughts flutter away as they danced.

He twirled her around the room, moving gracefully to the music, but Rose hardly noticed. They did not speak a word to each other, but it didn't matter. No words were necessary. Everything that they felt, everything that they needed to convey to the other, was there in their eyes. They understood each other. They felt the same thing—this utter wonderfulness of just being close to each other, of moving together as one.

Then there was silence. Rose felt herself reluctantly floating up from her blissful state. Had the music stopped?

Surely it had happened too quickly. What had happened to the dance? It seemed much too soon for it to be over.

Fungy took a step back and bowed to her. Purely through instinct, Rose returned it with her own curtsy. Her head felt like it was in a fog. She wasn't entirely sure where she was, or what she should be doing.

Luckily, Fungy was there. Without a word, he took her arm and gently led her outside onto the balcony. The fresh air and heady fragrance from the garden below awoke Rose to the reality of her situation.

She had just shared the most romantic dance with *Fungy!*

She had never thought of him as romantic before. In fact, quite the opposite. He was warm and comfortable. He was her friend.

And he was not someone with whom she should be sharing such feelings. It was wrong. She was going to marry Lord Kirtland.

Fungy leaned against the balustrade next to her, but Rose didn't look at him. She didn't need to. She could feel him. He wasn't nearly as close to her as he had been while they were dancing, but still she could feel his presence. She could smell his musky cologne and hear the rustle of his coat as it gently brushed against the wrought-iron railing.

She had never been so intensely aware of anyone before.

But what about Lord Kirtland? He had danced with her three times. She had made up her mind to marry him—and if she didn't after tonight, she would doubtless be labeled a loose-skirt, or worse.

But she couldn't ignore Fungy either. Finally, she forced herself to turn to him, intent on saying something that would indicate that their waltz had been a mistake, or to make some sort of joke about how she had completely lost herself in his arms.

The words died on her lips. He was looking at her with such a confused expression on his face that she nearly laughed. It was such a relief to see that he was as puzzled by what had just happened as she was.

"Rose . . . Miss Grace . . ." he began, when Aunt Farmington's voice intruded abruptly.

"Rose, you should not be out here alone, my girl!"

Rose felt her face heat, and spun around to address her aunt.

"We were, er . . ." she started.

"Just getting some fresh air, ma'am. After the exertion of the dance, Miss Grace felt the need for a breath of air." With Lady Farmington, Fungy had no problems finding his voice, and he took command of the situation with his usual aplomb.

"Yes, that is it. Nothing beyond that, Aunt Farmington, truly," Rose said gratefully.

"Ah, then you won't mind if I join you? It is quite a pleasant evening, isn't it? A little warm for this time of year, though," Aunt Farmington said as she stepped in between Rose and Fungy.

They each moved further apart to allow her room,

exchanging a quick glance. There was something that had needed to be said, but it would have to wait.

"Yes. It has been unseasonably warm," Fungy agreed.

"It makes it quite comfortable to wear these thin dresses that are all the rage, without the need for a shawl," the older lady said, rubbing one bare arm with her gloved hand.

"Are you chilled, ma'am? Shall I call someone to fetch your shawl?" Fungy asked.

Aunt Farmington narrowed her eyes at him, and then turned her intent scrutiny on Rose before answering. "No. No, I thank you. I shall send someone for it, and to find your father, Rose. I believe it is time we went home. You will join me in the foyer in five minutes."

"Yes, Aunt Farmington," Rose answered as her aunt left them alone once more on the balcony.

She then gave an embarrassed laugh. "She is turning into an excellent chaperone. She wasn't quite up to it when we first arrived, but now she is becoming quite the dragon."

Fungy gave a laugh. "Believe she sees more than you may realize. Older ladies have quite a talent for that."

An awkward silence hung between them for a moment. Somehow, the moment had passed, and Rose did not know how to bring it back.

"Well, goodnight," Fungy said at the same time as she said, "I should be going."

They both gave an embarrassed laugh, and Rose turned and sped away.


Fungy watched her go with a greater feeling of loss than he had ever experienced after saying goodnight to a young lady. He could not imagine what was getting into him.

First, he had been so amazingly inept at saying anything while they had danced, and then had not even been able to alleviate the awkward silence that had continued afterward.

But was it awkward? It had not seemed so during the dance. It had seemed right. Everything about that dance had seemed right.

Except perhaps for the fact that they were in public. The only thing that would have made it even more perfect was if they had been entirely alone.

My God, what was he thinking? Alone, with Miss Grace? It was a scandalous thought, and yet, so very enticing. In fact, he could think of nothing he would rather do than to get Miss Rose Grace alone and kiss her so thoroughly . . .

*No! Get hold of yourself, man. This is a proper young lady you are thinking of, not some harlot.*

But still the feeling lingered.

Fungy took a few deep cooling breaths of the heavily scented air. He needed to return to the ballroom. There were many more proper young ladies there with whom he should dance. It wasn't *so* late.

But none of them would be Rose.

# 16

Fungy stopped for a moment at the edge of the ball-room. He looked around at all of the hopeful young ladies who lined the walls, each standing next to their equally hopeful mamas.

They all looked so . . . uninteresting.

It would take a great deal of willpower to ask any one of them to dance tonight. After the waltz he had shared with Miss Grace, any other young woman would seem insipid.

"A true gentleman would not just stand by without asking a lady to dance, Sinjin," a soft, familiar voice said just behind him.

Fungy felt his heart stop. He turned around to find the past fifteen years of his life had faded away.

Georgiana stood just behind him.

She looked, if possible, even more beautiful than Fungy remembered. Her thick chestnut hair gleamed with luster in the candlelight, with just a few tendrils of curls allowed to surround her lovely face. Brown smiling eyes laughed at him, as did her full pink lips.

He took a step closer, feeling as if he was lost in a dream. Her familiar musky rose scent wafted over him like a warm summer day.

"Well? Will you not ask me to dance? Do I need to be so bold as to ask you?" she said, still laughing at him.

Fungy pulled himself together and made her a grand leg. "I would be grateful if you would honor me with this dance, my lady."

Her low chuckle washed over him as she held out her hand for him to take.

Gracefully, he swept her into his arms, thrilled that the orchestra was playing another waltz. Even after all these years, she felt as familiar to him as any woman could.

And yet there was something missing as he held her. He looked deeply at her face as she smiled up at him. There was perhaps a wrinkle or two that had not been there the last time he saw her, but other than that she was exactly the same.

So what had changed?

As he gently turned her about the room, he realized that it wasn't her, it was him. There was no tingle, no spark, no automatic tightening of his loins that he had always felt whenever he had seen her or held her. It just wasn't there. There was no sexual appeal, no feeling of anticipation, no thrill.

But how could this be? Could it be that he was still thinking about Rose?

Yes, that must be it. But how could he be thinking of her when he had Georgiana—his Georgiana— back in his arms? It used to be that he could not think of any other woman when he was with Georgiana. In fact, for so many years he had not been able to think of any other woman at all—with or without her. And yet, here he was, with no romantic feelings for her at all—this woman who had been his entire life and love.

Fungy's instinctive manners rescued him from revealing his sudden shocking discovery. He smiled down at her expectant face.

"Haven't changed, Georgiana. Not a bit."

"Tsk," she waved aside his compliment. "But you have, Sinjin." She moved back a bit in his arms and looked him over. "You are complete to a shade."

Fungy bowed his head. "Thank you."

"And from what I hear, you are quite the buck. Dictating fashions, setting all the girls atwitter with your attention, while getting the nod from the matrons as well. Quite well respected among the gentlemen, too."

"Please, making me blush!" Fungy said, a little embarrassed, but secretly thrilled that she had noticed. He felt like a student who had just received top marks in the class and had his work displayed for everyone to see—but the feeling was as platonic as that, as well.

"I've simply made myself into the man you wanted, Georgiana," Fungy said quietly, after regaining control of his pride.

Georgiana's eyes opened wide at this. "The man *I* wanted?"

"Told me the last day we were together. Said that you were marrying Mirthwood because I was not fashionable enough for you. I was not a member of the *haute ton*."

Georgiana thought about this, clearly dredging up the old memory. "Yes, I did, didn't I?"

"So, you see before you the man you wanted me to be."

She smiled at him, but the look in her eye was sad, as if she had lost something dear to her.

"How is Mirthwood?" Fungy asked

Georgiana's eyes looked up at his. "Have you not heard?" At his questioning look, she continued, "He died last year. The doctors believed it was cancer, but they couldn't be sure."

"I am terribly sorry."

Georgiana gave a gentle nod of her head in acceptance of his words. She then shrugged with a little half-smile on her lips. "So here I am. Back in London, returned to the bosom of society. Once again I am a widow, wondering if I want to try fate and marriage a third time."

# 17

The words were at the tip of his tongue: *Why don't you marry me, Georgiana?* But they wouldn't come out.

At one time, he would have said it in a trice. He would have said it without having to think about it even for a moment. But now he just could not make himself say the words, without the love and the passion he had once felt for her.

The dance ended. Georgiana took Fungy's arm, and he led her out onto the balcony where he had just been with Miss Grace.

Georgiana leaned out and looked into the garden below. "So, who is this young woman you have given your heart to?"

Fungy felt a rush of sheer shock run through him. But he made himself turn casually to look at her, leaning one hip against the balustrade. "Don't know what you mean."

She gave him a sly little smile. "Oh, come now, Sinjin. You need not be coy with me. I can tell. Now what is her name?"

"If you mean Miss Grace, I assure you . . ."

"Oh, please, Sinjin, if you begin to lie to me and take on these airs, I will simply wash my hands of you," she said, standing up and moving away from him.

Fungy turned toward the garden and leaned his hands on the railing. "Don't know that you could exactly call it love . . ."

"From the look I saw the two of you share while you danced, I would say it was love." She tapped him on his arm. "I know. I used to receive those looks too."

Fungy snapped his head back to look at her, but she didn't look sad or upset. In fact, she looked happy—happy for him.

But was she right? Was he, in fact, in love with Miss Grace? Was that what those feelings had been?

She nodded and put her hand gently on his sleeve. "It is all right, Sinjin. I believe it has been long enough, if not too long. I must say, I was truly surprised to hear that you hadn't married. But perhaps you were just waiting for the right young lady? And now, I take it, you believe this Miss Grace is the one worthy enough for your love?"

Fungy gave a little laugh. "She is more than worthy. I wonder if I am worthy enough for her. But as for love . . ."

"Sinjin! Don't tell me you were not aware of your feelings?"

Fungy stood silently, looking at Georgiana. She had always been so perceptive, such an excellent judge of character and of him in particular. He supposed that if she thought that he was in love with Miss Grace, it must be so. And, in fact, the more he thought about it, the more he thought that she might just be right.

Those feelings . . . losing himself with her as they had danced . . . He thought about it for a moment and then decided, that, yes, he *did* love Miss Grace.

"Tell me more about her," Georgiana demanded, bringing him back from his thoughts.

Fungy shrugged. "She is . . . sweet and innocent, and extremely intelligent. She is the daughter of Lord Pemberton-Howe, the archeologist."

Georgiana burst out laughing. "An archeologist! Why that is perfect for you, Sinjin. Couldn't be any better. Perhaps *she* will understand your funny classical quotes."

Fungy laughed. "Yes, I believe she would. Not only that, but she would know who said them and would have read them herself, in the original Greek."

"Oh, Sinjin. I am so happy for you. And I'm certain that with a girl like that you don't need all this." She indicated his clothes. "I'm sure that she loves you just as you are."

Fungy lost his smile. "I don't know that she loves me at all. And I have never shown her who I truly am. To her, I am merely Fungy, and a dandy."

"But surely you've quoted your sayings to her? She knows that you enjoy all of those classical books you are forever reading?"

Fungy shook his head. "No, Georgiana. I stopped reading them for a while. In fact, it was meeting Miss Grace that inspired me to pick them up again."

He paused and then added quietly, "I think even my closest friends have forgotten."

Georgiana placed her hand on his arm. "Oh, Sinjin. I am sorry. But you should not let this stop you from pursuing this young lady. *Show* her who you are. Let her meet Sinjin—the real you. You know that she will love you for it. Unlike silly women like me, she will appreciate not only your physical beauty, but the beauty of your mind as well."

"I . . ."

"Sinjin, you know that you love her, and I know that she sounds absolutely perfect for you. What are you waiting for?"

"For you," he whispered, his voice not quite working. "I was waiting for you, Georgiana. Whether you meant to or not, you *did* take my heart with you when you left."

She gave him a little smile. "Then let me give it back to you, Sinjin, so that you may give it to Miss Grace."

He nodded, and then took his old love in his arms, feeling her supple curves against his chest, but knowing that he felt nothing for her.

No, that wasn't true—what he felt for her were the greatest respect and friendship.

Rose woke up to find her sisters breathing down her neck.

She cracked one eye open, saw Thalia's face within inches of her own, and immediately closed her eye again.

"I saw that!" Thalia said.

Rose turned over, and came face to face with Laia who was resting her elbow on Rose's pillow, watching her. They had her surrounded.

She turned onto her stomach.

"You can't hide from us, Rose. Time for your report," Thalia sang into her ear.

Rose lifted her pillow to hide her head under, but it was snatched from her hands before she could do so.

"Oh no, you don't. We want to know about the ball last night."

"C'mon Rose, tell us. Did you dance with Fungy?"

"Did you dance with Lord Kirtland?"

"Were you the most fashionably dressed girl there?"

"Does Lord Kirtland play any sport, did you find out?"

"Were there any other interesting gentlemen, perhaps a little younger, who might be interested in a girl not quite out yet?"

Rose groaned and threw her arm over her face. "Why can't you two at least wait until I've woken up before you barrage me with questions?"

"That wouldn't be any fun," Thalia said.

"And we want to know now. If we let you wake up, you might forget to tell us later. And, besides, Aunt Farmington will be in the drawing room later, so you won't be able to give us any of the fun details, like how many times you danced with Fungy," Laia said, sitting up and crossing her legs in front of her, while placing Rose's pillow across her lap.

Rose snatched her pillow back. Putting it behind her, she sat up and leaned back against it.

"Well, did you dance with Lord Kirtland?" Laia asked once again, with great expectation on her face.

Rose smiled at her sister, unable to hide her pleasure. "I did. We danced *three* times."

"Three times? Is that a lot?" Thalia asked.

"Yes, it is. It means that he is serious about wanting to marry me. Only people who are engaged or married dance together so many times."

"Are you engaged to him?" Thalia asked.

"No. But I imagine I will be soon. He needs only to ask."

"But what about Fungy?" Laia asked.

"When do you think he will ask you?" Thalia asked at the same time.

"I don't know when he'll ask," Rose answered her youngest sister. "And Fungy is just a friend, Laia. I've explained that to you already."

Deliberately, she turned her mind away from her memories of the dance they had shared together. That dance had no place in her current plans.

"But I thought you liked him."

"I do like him. I like him very much." Rose slipped past her sisters and got out of bed.

"So you should marry Fungy! Why don't you marry him?" Laia said, snatching her pillow back again and holding it close to her.

Rose picked up her wrap and put it on slowly, and allowed herself to briefly think about Fungy. He had made her feel good last night, very good. Never had she felt more comfortable and happy with anyone. She could still feel the sensations from the special magic that they had shared during their dance.

Magic. Yes, that is definitely what it was. A few moments' enchantment.

But it was Lord Kirtland who would provide the opportunity for her to work in Egypt and Greece for the rest of her life, as well as the money her family desperately needed right now.

She turned around and faced her sisters. "Fungy is a good friend and I care for him a great deal. I feel the same for him as I do for the two of you. In fact, better—he's not as annoying as you are."

Thalia laughed.

"But that is what makes him perfect," Laia said.

"Just imagine how much fun we would all have together," Thalia said, adding her voice to her sister's argument.

It was true, Rose thought for a moment. They would all have a grand time together.

But there was more to marriage than just that. She shook her head. "Fungy doesn't make me feel the same way that Lord Kirtland does."

"How does Lord Kirtland make you feel, Rose?" Laia asked.

Rose shrugged her shoulders and smiled. "All shivery and nervous. With Fungy, I only feel comfortable. He makes me feel good, but he doesn't put me on edge like Lord Kirtland does. I am certain that I am in love with Lord Kirtland, and nothing more than good friends with Fungy. And besides, Lord Kirtland has so much more to recommend him as a husband—he is rich and an archeologist, besides being quite handsome."

Laia sighed, and then gave a little shrug of her shoulders as if resigning herself to this. "Well, then, how are you going to get him to propose?"

Rose sat down on the edge of her bed. "I don't know. I really have no idea what else I can do to let him know that I would be open to a proposal. I danced with him three times in one night, I've gone on an outing with him . . ." Rose shrugged. "What else can I do?"

"You could ask Fungy. I bet he would know," Thalia suggested.

Both Rose and Laia turned to look at their youngest sister. "No!" said Rose at the same time that Laia said, "That is the worst idea I have ever heard."

"Why? I'm sure he would know what Rose needs to do to get Lord Kirtland to propose."

"I could *never* ask Fungy!"

"But you just said what a good friend he was. If he's such a good friend, why can't you ask him?"

Rose thought about this for a minute. Thalia did have a point there. And she was certainly right in that he would know what to do. "I still don't like it. It's not proper." She shook her head and then began to get up.

"Well, if you don't ask him, then I will," Thalia said, crossing her arms over her chest.

"Thalia!" Laia exclaimed.

"Thalia, you wouldn't!" Rose protested.

"Oh yes I would. And he is coming here today. He sent 'round a note asking if you would be at home. I believe that Aunt Farmington answered it already, saying that you would be."

Rose gasped. Fungy was coming to pay her a visit? Why? She hoped it wouldn't have anything to do with what had been left unsaid after their dance. "All right, Thalia, I will ask him, but I still don't think it is right."

# 18

A knock sounded on Rose's door.

She got up and quickly finished tying her wrap around her waist as her father came into the room. He didn't look as if he had slept much the previous night, but there was an odd light in his eyes nonetheless.

"Ah, you are all here. Good."

"Good morning, Papa," the three girls said in unison.

He gave them a smile. "Good morning, my three graces." He patted Rose on the cheek. "I have to go out of town for a few days, Rosebud. You will please look after your sisters?"

"Where are you going?" Thalia asked.

"I always look after them, Papa," Rose said.

"Eh? Oh, I've got to go to Pemberton. Ran into our old neighbor Squire Thompson last night at Whites. Told me an interesting bit of news."

He smiled, half to himself. "Aunt Farmington will be here, of course. Don't know when I'll be back. Be good," he admonished his two younger daughters.

And then before they could ask any more questions, he left.

The three girls just looked at each other.

"I don't believe I've seen him so excited since we were in Greece," Rose said finally.

"Is that what that was, excitement?" Thalia asked.

"He looked very tired to me," Laia said.

"He did look tired, but he always looks tired when he's excited. He used to stay up all night examining his books and checking his facts before finally going down to the excavation and discovering something wonderful—at least that's what he did in Greece." Rose shrugged her shoulders.

"But what could he find at Pemberton?" Thalia asked.

"I have no idea. I suppose we'll find out when he returns."


Sinjin followed the butler into the Graces' drawing room.

One look at Miss Grace and he knew immediately that Georgiana had been right. She was not only beautiful and intelligent, but just being with her made him happy. It had been so long since he had felt this way about a woman that he hadn't recognized his love for her when it was directly in front of him.

He had spent most of the night thinking about all that Georgiana had said. And he knew now what he must do.

Just as he had put aside Sinjin so many years ago, he had to take him up again. He wanted—no, needed—to recapture that exuberance for life, that passion for learning, that drive for . . . well, everything that he had had as a young man. He wanted to *be* Sinjin once more.

And it would all begin with Rose.

"Mr. Fotheringay-Phipps, Miss Grace," the butler intoned. "I shall inform Lady Farmington that you have a guest."

"If you don't mind, Miss Grace, I would prefer it if we could have some privacy," Sinjin said quickly.

The butler looked to his mistress for direction. She looked a little surprised at this, but then nodded. "An excellent idea. Do not worry, Reynolds, we shall leave the door open, and my sisters are nearby if I need any assistance."

The butler gave Sinjin a warning look before bowing himself out of the room.

He moved forward and handed Rose the bouquet of roses he had brought.

"Although not nearly as lovely as you, I could not resist the temptation," he said.

Rose flushed prettily. "Thank you."

She pulled the bell, and when the maid came, she handed her the flowers and instructed her to put them into a vase.

"It is so nice that you could come to visit, Fungy," Rose said, as she sat down in a chair by the empty fireplace, indicating for him to take the opposite chair.

"I would be honored if you would call me Sinjin, Miss Grace. It is my given name," he said, sitting down.

"Oh!" Rose gave a little embarrassed laugh. "Isn't it funny? I never thought of you having a Christian name since you are called Fungy by everyone. But of course, Fungy is just a short form of Fotheringay-Phipps."

"Yes. Sinjin, spelled St. John, of course, is my given name. An unfortunate name, but mine, nonetheless."

"It is no more unfortunate than Euphrosyne, I assure you."

Sinjin laughed. "No, suppose not. But Rose is a beautiful name, and fits you very well. Would you mind if I called you by your given name?"

"No. Not at all. I would be honored," she said, flushing a very pretty pink.

He wasn't exactly sure where one started a marriage proposal. Was he supposed to get down on one knee right away and tell her of his undying love?

No, that didn't seem right. He should ease into it perhaps.

"Last night, Rose, I enjoyed your company a great deal," he began, awkwardly.

"As did I enjoy yours."

"The waltz . . ."

"Yes! It was very . . ."

"Special." Sinjin finished for her.

"Indeed."

Sinjin felt as if his heart would burst with joy. She had felt it too. She had felt the magic, the love, that incredible moment they had had together. But how could she not? It was so strong, so tangible.

Vestiges of the desire he had felt for her after their dance still played throughout his body. To hold her in his arms, feel her sweet lips against his, and, oh, so much more! The thought was making him distinctly uncomfortable.

But she was saying something and he had missed the beginning of it.

". . . such a good friend, er, Sinjin. I know that I can trust you."

"Of course!" he said quickly, as she paused for breath.

She smiled at him warmly. "Then, perhaps, since you are such a good friend, you wouldn't mind giving me a little advice? I have a small . . . dilemma."

Sinjin returned her smile. "You know that you can ask anything of me."

"It is just . . ." she suddenly seemed very uncomfortable. Studying her hands in her lap, she said, "There is a . . ." A blush crept up her cheeks as she struggled to find the words. ". . . a gentleman of whom I am particularly fond."

Sinjin felt his heart begin to beat a little faster.

*I knew it! I knew it! She felt my love for her and wants to tell me that she feels the same way.*

Sinjin tried to control the smile on his face, and masked it with a look of concern for her "dilemma."

"I . . . I'm afraid I am unsure of how to tell him how I feel. I do not wish to be too bold . . ."

"No, of course not. Completely understand your problem. It is a difficult situation for a proper young lady to be in." Sinjin silently congratulated himself for his restraint when all he wanted to do was to throw himself at her feet and assure her that he loved her too. He crossed his knee over his other leg, careful not to scratch his well-polished boots, and clenched his hands together in his lap.

"And yet, I am not sure what I can do to—to show the gentleman that I am interested—that I would welcome . . ." Her cheeks were fiery red by now. Poor girl was really having troubles.

Sinjin felt sorry for her, but he would be patient just a little longer. He did not want to startle her or put her off by his own eagerness.

"Is it a proposal of marriage that you would welcome?" Sinjin asked gently, while having the hardest time keeping still.

She stole a look up at him, but immediately refocused on her hands in her lap. She gave him a little nod.

"Well, then . . ." he began.

"It is just that I think I have done all that I can to—to let him know how I feel," she interrupted.

"Are you certain?" Sinjin asked, just to tease her, and himself, a little bit further. He knew her relief would be great when she learned of his reason for coming to visit her today. They would have a great laugh over this for many years to come.

"Oh yes, why, I even danced with him three times last night!"

"Three times?" Sinjin's heart began to slow, and a chill crept over his whole body.

He and Rose had only danced together the one time last night. It was indeed a memorable dance, but it was only one.

"Yes. You would think that a gentleman so intelligent as to be an archeologist would understand my intentions, but I'm worried that he may not have. Am I just being silly? Perhaps I should be more patient."

*Archeologist?*

Sinjin was not sure, but he thought his heart may have stopped beating altogether.

She was not speaking of him.

He was not the man she wanted to marry. She didn't love him.

# 19

Sinjin took a moment to digest this. It was not easy. Already, there was a growing ache inside of his chest.

If it was not him whom she loved, then who was it? Who had she danced with three times last night?

The answer came quickly enough, even to Sinjin's numb mind. Lord Kirtland.

His Rose was in love with Lord Kirtland.

After so many years of protecting himself, of avoiding all romantic situations, of making sure that no woman could ever come near to breaking his heart the way Georgiana had, he had finally opened himself up.

And this is what he got.

Sinjin almost laughed at the irony. He also almost cried, so acute was the pain.

He stood up and turned toward the door. He had to go. He had to leave before he unmanned himself. Before he displayed even the smallest bit of what he was feeling.

"Fungy? Are you all right?" Rose stood up as well.

"What? Yes. Yes, of course. I am sorry, Miss Grace, I just thought of . . . of an appointment that I am late for.

"Regarding Lord Kirtland—yes, I would advise patience. As you say, he is an intelligent man. I am certain that he is merely waiting for the right opportunity to . . . to make his intentions clear. Good day, Miss Grace."

Without even turning around to face her, he strode from the room as quickly as he could. There was nothing else he could do. He could not even summon up his usual witty reply.

Rose just stood there and watched him leave.

Why had he done that?

Rose sat down on the sofa, thinking furiously. The brief look of pain that had crossed his face—for a moment she had thought it must have been her imagination.

But no, it hadn't been, she realized this now. The knowledge that she had been referring to Lord Kirtland as the man she was willing to marry had come to Fungy slowly and, quite possibly, painfully.

Rose got up and began pacing back and forth, furiously kicking the hem of her dress in front of her as her stride lengthened.

He had been upset. He had been mortally upset by her thoughtless question. How could she have done this? How could she have hurt the man she cared for so much? Who, clearly, cared for her much more, although in a very different way. That was clear to her now.

Fungy loved her.

And she had just told him that she was in love with someone else!

Rose dropped back down onto the sofa once more.

It was so obvious. He *must* be in love with her. Why else would he have rescued her so many times? Why else would he have looked at her in that way at the ball last night while they danced? Why else had he been so sweet and kind to her at the card party, and at the park—not to mention all of the other times he had rescued her or her sisters from their own folly?

And now as thanks, she had been unbearably cruel to him.

Tears began trickling down Rose's face, but she did nothing to stop them.

*Oh, how could she have done this!*

She felt the warmth of another hand grasp onto hers. Looking up, she saw Laia at her side. She was joined a moment later by Thalia.

"What has happened?" "Rose, are you all right?" the two girls said in unison.

Rose rested her head against Laia's shoulder, but said nothing. Her throat was still too constricted with shame to be able to say anything just yet.

Laia soothed her hair while Thalia took Rose's hand and held it comfortingly.

"Was it Fungy? Was he mean to you? What did he say?" Laia asked.

"Did you ask him about Lord Kirtland?"

"Did he say it was hopeless?"

Rose sniffed and sat up again wiping away the tears from her cheeks. "He was not mean to me. It was I who was cruel beyond words to him."

"What do you mean? What happened?"

Rose told her sisters exactly what had happened, from the moment Fungy had walked into the room to the time when he left it so abruptly.

They were silent for a few minutes after, each digesting what she had told them.

"So you think that he loves you?" Thalia finally asked, quietly.

"Of course he does! Weren't you listening?" Laia asked her little sister scornfully.

"Please, Laia, do not be hurtful," Rose said, laying a hand gently on Laia's knee. "Yes, Thalia, I believe that he does—and that I have hurt him a great deal by telling him about my affection for Lord Kirtland. Whatever must he think of me?"

"But it was not your fault," Thalia objected.

"Yes, it was Thalia who suggested that you tell him," Laia added.

Rose shook her head sadly. "No. It is entirely my fault. I should not have taken her advice. I knew it was wrong and now I have my just reward. It is Fungy who I am worried about now."

The girls were silent once more, until Laia asked, "What are you going to do, Rose?"

Rose shook her head. "I don't know."

Her head had begun pounding with pain as she had retold her tale to her sisters. Now, it was becoming increasingly unbearable.

"I think I will lie down for a bit. I have the most awful migraine. Later, I will figure out what to do." Rose got up slowly and walked up to her room. Her sisters did not even try to follow her. For once, they respected her pain and allowed her her privacy.


As the three sisters sat subdued at breakfast the following morning, Reynolds entered the dining room with a note for Rose.

"What is it, Rose?" Aunt Farmington asked, as soon as she had broken open the seal.

"Who is it from?" Thalia said, around a mouthful of egg.

Rose wiped at the tears that began to slide down her cheeks as she read the note.

Laia snatched it from her limp hand and read out loud.

*Dear Miss Grace,*
    *Thinking over your dilemma, I have come to the conclusion that what is needed is an Opportunity. Therefore,*

*I will be hosting a small party at Kensington Gardens this coming Friday. No word of the purpose of the gathering will be told to anyone. It will simply be an afternoon of pleasure for a few close friends of mine.*

   *I do hope that this date is convenient for you.*
      *Sincerely,*
      *Your good friend,*
      *St. John Fotheringay-Phipps*

"What is the purpose of the party?" Aunt Farmington asked. "What dilemma do you have, my dear?"

Rose wiped her eyes with her napkin. "How to get Lord Kirtland to propose to me," she said quietly.

Aunt Farmington's eyes widened.

Thalia quickly brought Aunt Farmington up to date on what had happened the previous afternoon.

Aunt Farmington shook her head. "You told a gentleman that you were in love with someone else?"

"I did not know he loved me!" Rose protested.

"I am extremely disappointed in you, Rose. The nerve . . . how could you?" She paused in her horror to pick up Fungy's note and reread it. "Well, you have no choice but to attend this little gathering of Fungy's, since he is holding it for you."

"Yes. I shall reply to him immediately."

"And you shall thank him most sincerely!" Aunt Farmington said sternly.

"Yes, ma'am. No need to remind me of that."

"I have never heard of such cheekiness! And to get away with it, is by all that is . . ."

"Please Aunt Farmington, please don't make this any worse," Rose pleaded.

"Oh yes, ma'am, I assure you Rose knows that what she did was wrong, and has been berating herself for it since yesterday," Laia said, trying to be helpful.

Aunt Farmington, however, just frowned at all three girls.

\* \* \*

"Sinjin, this was a wonderful idea," Georgiana said, taking a sip of her wine. She was looking, if possible, even more lovely than she had at the ball. Her rich rust-colored walking dress brought out the warmth in her eyes, and she wore a very fetching bonnet. She looked completely relaxed on the blanket that had been laid on the soft grass for her and the other ladies.

"Yes, indeed, Fungy. My goodness, I can't believe how long it's been since we were all together like this," Teresa, Lady Merrick, said. She was sitting near Georgiana, and held a parasol so as to protect her fair skin from the harmful rays of the sun.

Sinjin stood up. "Well, then, a toast. To old friends." He raised his glass toward Georgiana, as well as to Merry, Sin, Julian and their wives.

"And to new," he continued, raising his glass toward Rose and Lord Kirtland.

"Hear, hear!" many said, while others echoed, "To friends!"

"Well, I, for one, think that Fungy invited us all here just so that we could admire his new way of tying his neckcloth!" Cassandra, Lady Huntley, said with a touch of laughter in her voice.

"Yes, Fungy, what do you call that style?" Julian asked, while absently tugging at one of his wife's blond curls which had escaped from the knot on top of her head. They made a striking pair, her fair English loveliness a perfect contrast to his dark-skinned good looks.

Sinjin gave a little bow, pleased that his friends had noticed this exceptional new way of tying his neckcloth that he had created just that morning. "Call it the Friendship knot—in honor of the occasion, of course."

"It looks unusually simple. Did it take you hours to

achieve?" Sara, Lady Reath, asked, leaning forward her diminutive frame so that she could get a better look.

"But, of course," Sinjin answered, with mock surprise.

"What a question! Fungy always takes hours over his neckcloth," Merry said, laughing.

"*Au contraire*, my esteemed cousin," Sinjin began.

"No, I was quite impressed. It only took him twenty minutes that last time I was present at the event," Julian interrupted.

"Only twenty minutes?" Sin asked, disbelievingly, but with a laugh in his voice.

"Why don't you spend so much time on your neckcloth, Sin? Maybe then you could look bang up to the mark like Fungy." His wife laughed.

"What a waste of time," Lord Kirtland said quietly.

"Ah, but not if you care to make a good impression on the ladies, Lord Kirtland," Georgiana said, turning around to look at him. "I am just surprised that my dear old friend Sinjin, who could barely be bothered to button his waistcoat when I last saw him, would now spend the time necessary to make such an impression."

"Always dressed properly!" Sinjin protested.

"Yes, perhaps, but only just barely so," she grudgingly admitted to the guffaws of Sinjin's friends.

"I can't imagine him not dressed to perfection," Rose said.

"No, nor can I," Sara agreed.

"He's always been impeccably attired since I've known him," Teresa added.

"You ladies did not know me in my salad days, that is all," Sinjin said.

"I remember those days," Merry said.

"I prefer to forget them," Sin put in.

Everyone burst out laughing once more.

"Well, it is a lovely day," Sinjin said, stepping toward the ladies. "I am going take the beautiful Lady Mirthwood for a walk, if she would so honor me?" He held out his hand to help Georgiana up.

Before offering his arm to Georgiana, Sinjin watched out of the corner of his eye as Rose took Lord Kirtland's proffered arm.

It killed him to think that he would be the one responsible for enabling the woman he loved to marry another. And yet, what could he do? If she loved Kirtland, there was nothing Sinjin could do to make her love him instead.

On the other hand, if Kirtland did not take advantage of this golden opportunity that Sinjin had just dropped into his lap, then it would prove that he was not worthy of her affections.

In that case, there would be nothing stopping Sinjin from doing all that he could to secure Rose's affection. If Kirtland didn't propose today, he would be a bigger fool than Sinjin could believe possible.

"Do you wish to follow them, Sinjin?"

"What?"

"I think you are going to strain your neck if you continue to watch Miss Grace walk in that direction, while we are walking this way. However, if you wish, we could follow them."

Sinjin felt his face heat with embarrassment. He had not meant to be so obvious, and he had not meant to ignore Georgiana either. "No, not at all. You must forgive me—I was merely distracted for a moment. Although how I could be so, when I have the most beautiful and fascinating woman present with me, I honestly don't know."

"Ah yes, that is why I used to put up with you so long ago—you are the most atrociously wonderful flirt I have ever had the privilege to know!"

Sinjin laughed and then gave Georgiana a magnificent leg in acceptance of her accusation. "Too kind, Georgiana, as always, you are too kind."

# 20

"I am happy that you are feeling better," Lord Kirtland said, as they strolled slowly across the grass. "I was quite worried when I received your note Tuesday afternoon to say that you were too ill to attend the card party."

"Thank you. It was just a temporary ailment," Rose said, trying to remain calm. Ever since Fungy had stood up and announced that he was going to take Lady Mirthwood for a walk, Rose felt as if her heart had been lodged in her throat.

This was it. This was the opportunity for Lord Kirtland to get her alone and to propose.

"It is a shame that it kept you from the party. Aiken won a monkey from George Cole. It was quite exciting to watch them play. Cole, you know, is very good."

"Oh yes? I am very sorry to have missed it," Rose said. However, if things worked out as she hoped this afternoon, she need never attend another card party again.

Rose did not imagine this to be a great hardship. Although she loved the thrill of playing, she did not relish the agony of owing money as she did even now.

"I was looking forward to giving you the opportunity to win back the money you owe me from last week's party."

"That is kind of you," Rose said, but not particularly kind of Lord Kirtland to remind her of her debt. Rose mentally shook her head. She would think nothing but good thoughts of Lord Kirtland today. Today was a special day.

He was going to propose. She knew he would. It was what had kept her stomach feeling like it was tied up in knots all day. If all went right, she would soon be engaged to this man. Rose took a deep calming breath and gave Lord Kirtland a little smile.

*What if he didn't propose?* Rose almost stopped walking as this horrible thought echoed in her mind. She forced herself to continue on, however, as if nothing was wrong. But what would she do? All of Fungy's hard work would be for nothing, her family would be ruined, she would need to find another gentleman to marry quickly—she might even be forced to marry someone old and smelly. Rose nearly shuddered at the thought.

And following this dreadful thought was one that scared her even more—what would she do if he *did* propose?

It was what she wanted, she was completely certain of that now. But it didn't make her any less scared. She was in love with Lord Kirtland, she reminded herself. And he was the key to her family's future, thanks to his wealth.

No, it was going to be fine. Absolutely fine. They would have a wonderful life together excavating archeological ruins. They would be a team, just like her own parents had been. It would be wonderful.

But still, her stomach refused to relax.

They came to a large folly, which provided a very nice respite from the heat of the day. Although Rose had remembered to bring her parasol, she was still quite warm. That, combined with her nerves, made her feel a bit uncomfortable, but the folly was lovely and cool.

Sitting down on the cold stone bench, Rose looked out at the broad green lawns that stretched on for what looked like nearly a mile before dropping down to a very pretty ornamental lake.

As she was sitting sideways on the bench facing the lake, she didn't see Lord Kirtland sit down behind her. But she was very much aware of him. Just knowing that he was sitting so very close to her sent shivers down her spine.

She held tightly onto the handle of her parasol, hoping that Lord Kirtland wouldn't notice her shaking fingers.

"Miss Grace." Lord Kirtland placed his hand on top of hers. "Perhaps I presume too much, but may I say that I find you an extremely attractive young lady?"

Rose turned around and looked into Lord Kirtland's dark eyes. He was looking very serious and not a little forbidding, as he always did when he drew his eyebrows down over his deep-set brown eyes.

She swallowed hard. He was probably as nervous as she was, she thought.

"Thank you, my lord," Rose managed to say.

"I find you attractive not only in your physical beauty, but in the beauty of your mind as well. And as we both have a great love of archeology, I believe that we would suit uncommonly well."

"I completely agree!" Rose blurted out.

Lord Kirtland laughed, and seemed to relax a little. "Just think of the archeological expeditions we could embark on together if we married. With your father's connections and no financial worries, we could go to Egypt and join in the work of exploring more of the fabulous tombs there—perhaps finding more gold jewelry and priceless sarcophagi."

"I did love Egypt. The tombs are filled with such fascinating hieroglyphs and paintings," Rose agreed.

"May I speak with your father, then?"

"Oh, yes, my lord, as soon as he returns from the country," Rose breathed as she watched Lord Kirtland's face come closer to her own.

This time she did not flinch or turn away, but forced herself not to move while he gently pressed his lips to hers.

It was an odd sensation, his lips and breath so hot against her face. There were no tingles, as she had expected, but rather a chill that brought goose bumps to her arms. Rose didn't understand it, but she supposed that this is what it felt like when one was in love.

She tried kissing him back, but didn't want to seem too bold. And honestly, she was not entirely sure what to do.

Finally, he moved back. She gave him a nervous little smile, and then looked down at her hands still clutching her parasol. Hopefully, he was happy with her attempt, but she was really too nervous to even look at his face to see.

But it was over. It was done! He had proposed and she had accepted. He now only needed to make the arrangements with her father and everything would be settled.

The relief was overwhelming! All of a sudden, Rose felt like she could breathe again, and she had the overwhelming urge to throw her arms around Lord Kirtland's neck and laugh for the sheer joy of knowing that everything was going to be all right now.

Everything was going to be absolutely perfect!

Rose nearly giggled.

Lord Kirtland would forgive her gaming debts, he would pay their bills, and she would have the money she would need to see her sisters launched into society properly.

Hopefully, she would be able to return to England for Laia's coming out. Although being on an archeological dig again would be wonderful, and she was truly looking forward to going back to Egypt, she also knew that she would be needed to keep Laia in line and could possibly even give her some pointers on how to behave properly in society.

Rose nearly did laugh out loud at that thought— she, Rose Grace, telling another how to behave properly in society.

She caught Lord Kirtland's eye. He gave her a questioning little smile. "I am very glad that you are happy about this."

A giggle finally did escape from her mouth. "Yes, my lord, I am very happy. You are too, I hope?" Rose asked quickly.

"Yes, my dear. Very happy," he said. And indeed, he did look happy—although relieved, perhaps, would have been a more accurate description for the expression on his face. Rose supposed that he had been just as nervous as she was. But now everything was just as it ought to be.

If only Rose didn't have this feeling of unease in the pit of her stomach. Well, she was sure that it would go away as she got to know Lord Kirtland better.

# 21

"Oh, what a lovely aspect." Lady Mirthwood's voice was saying rather loudly as she and Fungy stepped into the folly. "I have so missed English gardens. You know they try to copy them in America, but somehow, they just aren't the same."

Lord Kirtland immediately stood up and moved away from Rose, as if they had been caught kissing.

Rose was grateful for the interruption and the company.

Although she was not entirely sure how much she liked Lady Mirthwood—she was entirely too familiar with Fungy—but right now she would have welcomed almost anyone. And she did so want to share the news with Fungy. His plan had worked to perfection, just as she had known it would.

"Lord Kirtland, Miss Grace. Didn't see you here. Please excuse us for interrupting," Fungy said, stopping just inside the folly.

"It is no problem. None at all. We . . . ah, well, you may be the first to congratulate us. Miss Grace has just consented to become my wife."

Rose stood up, looking at Fungy perhaps closer than was polite. Did he seem upset? Yes, she decided, he most certainly did, but just for a fleeting moment. Now he was hiding it manfully.

Rose bit the inside of her lip. She didn't wish to say anything that might further his hurt, but she did so desperately want to thank him.

"Congratulations," Lady Mirthwood said, pulling Rose's attention away from Fungy. She gave Rose a little smile that didn't quite reach her eyes. Somehow, she didn't seem as happy as Rose would have expected.

Did Lady Mirthwood know of Fungy's infatuation with Rose? Was that why her reaction was so subdued? She must. But then, why wasn't she happy? She could have Fungy all to herself now—if that was what she wanted. And judging by the way she behaved with him, in such an obviously intimate way, Rose couldn't imagine that Lady Mirthwood would not have been very pleased by this news.

Rose was not jealous, she reassured herself, she just wished Lady Mirthwood would not be so conspicuous.

Fungy tried to put a little more animation in his response to the news from Rose and Lord Kirtland. As if abruptly coming to life, he said, "Excellent! Lucky man."

He reached out and took Lord Kirtland's hand, pumping it up and down. "So happy for you, Miss Grace." He then took Rose's hand and simply pressed it meaningfully between both of his, looking deeply into her eyes.

The heat from his hand shot up her arm and sent tingles running through Rose's veins, immediately dispelling her chills of a few moments ago.

Rose gave him her most grateful look, trying to convey her thanks to him for what he had done. She was deeply indebted to him.

He understood, for his smile softened and he gave her a little nod.

\* \* \*

Georgiana was unusually quiet on the way home after the picnic. Sinjin didn't mind. He had enough to think about himself.

He had to admit that he had been disappointed, though not at all surprised, that Kirtland had come through. He had hoped that he would not, but now that he thought about it, he knew that it had been an unreasonable hope. If he were in Kirtland's place, he would have jumped at the opportunity to propose to Rose without a moment's hesitation—just as Kirtland had.

No, Kirtland was no fool, that was certain.

Georgiana's warm hand on his own startled Sinjin from his thoughts. She gave him a consoling smile.

She knew. Naturally, she had known right away that Sinjin had been in love with Rose, even before he had realized it himself. And now she knew just how upset he was that she had become engaged to another.

How silly of him to try and hide anything from her. She knew him so well. Better, in fact, than he knew himself at times.

He pulled up to her townhouse and then jumped down to help her descend from his phaeton.

"Would you mind if I stepped inside with you for a moment?" he asked, suddenly knowing exactly what he must do.

She smiled up at him. "I would like that."

As they entered the neat little house, Georgiana instructed her footman to take care of Sinjin's equipage for a short time. Sinjin gave him a nod, and then followed Georgiana up to her drawing room.

She immediately poured him a glass of brandy and then took some wine for herself, sitting down on a pink scroll-back sofa. Sinjin took a fortifying sip, and then took a deep breath as he set the glass aside.

Instead of taking the seat she offered to him, he knelt

at her feet and took her free hand in his own. "Georgiana, I would be honored if you would marry me."

The room was immediately filled with the beautiful sound of Georgiana's laughter. That is, until she looked into his eyes and saw that he was utterly serious.

"Oh, Sinjin." She ran her hand along his cheek in a motherly fashion. "I know that you are upset over Miss Grace, but truly, this is not the answer."

"I am not doing this because of Miss Grace," Sinjin said, standing up again. "I have been thinking of this ever since we met at the ball the other night," he lied.

It would not do to let her know that she had hit the nail right on the head. And what were a few little lies, when it ensured that he would not die alone and unloved by anyone?

"I simply do not believe I could stand by and watch you marry someone else yet again. You are too beautiful and too special a woman to live as a widow for very long. I know that if I do not ask you now, it will be too late and I will have missed what may have been my last opportunity to have you for my very own."

Georgiana stood up. Putting down her own drink, she put her arms around Sinjin's neck and kissed him deeply.

He tasted the wine on her tongue and the sweetness of her mouth. That, coupled with the feel of her luscious body pressed against his, should have sent shivers of excitement through him.

But it did not. He felt nothing—nothing but the remnants of what used to be his great love for this woman, now a great platonic love and friendship.

Was it enough to last him the rest of his life? He supposed it had to be. It was the only choice he had. He deepened his kiss, but felt her pull away.

"My dearest Sinjin," she smiled up at him. "You know that I cannot marry a man who is in love with someone else—not even if that man is you."

"But . . ."

Georgiana pressed her finger to his lips. "No. You cannot deny it, my dear. I can feel it. I am sorry she is engaged to marry Lord Kirtland, and not just for your sake."

Sinjin stopped as he was about to reach down to pick up his glass of brandy. "What do you mean?" he said, straightening up again.

Georgiana gave a little shrug. "I'm not entirely sure, but there is something about Lord Kirtland. I don't know if it is because he is wrong for Miss Grace, or if it is something about him personally, but something about their engagement just rubs me the wrong way."

Sinjin sat down with his drink. "No, it is Kirtland. I'm sure of it. I've had bad feelings about him ever since I met him. At first, I just thought it was jealousy, but now I am beginning to think otherwise."

"Well, whatever it is, I just hope Miss Grace realizes it before it is too late for her."

This worried Sinjin more than he could say, and it seemed that Georgiana felt the same way.

His dear, sweet Rose could get trapped into marriage with this fellow for the rest of her life—it was a terrifying thought.


"Well done! That is excellent news," Aunt Farmington said after Rose bounded into the drawing room and announced her engagement. "Girls, why do you not congratulate your sister? You should be very happy for her."

"Congratulations, Rose," Laia said with almost no emotion whatsoever in her voice.

Thalia showed a bit more emotion. She frowned at Rose, while saying, "I am very happy for you, Rose."

"My, what excitement and joy!" Rose said, unexpectedly feeling like a balloon that had released all of its air. Deflated, she dropped down on the sofa. "I thought that you would both be happy for me."

"We are!" Laia exclaimed, moving over and giving her sister a hug. "We just hope that you are doing the right thing. Marrying the right man."

"We truly want you to be happy, Rose," Thalia said coming over and sitting at her sister's feet.

Rose gave her sisters' hands a squeeze. "I know you do, and I *will* be happy. Lord Kirtland is definitely the right man. He is everything I could possibly want in a husband. I've explained this to you before."

"Yes, it is just . . ."

"I know what it is," Rose interrupted her sister. "You simply don't know Lord Kirtland. I am certain that if you got to know him better, you would be just as thrilled as I am."

She jumped up and strode over to the escritoire. Pulling out a sheet of paper, she said, "I shall write him a note asking him to come and meet you both. I just know that after you have met him, you will like him and be happy for us."

# 22

A ride in the park wasn't exactly what Rose had had in mind for her sisters' first meeting with Lord Kirtland. But she was happy that her sisters would be able to spend a little time with her new fiancé, even if it was in a public setting.

"Oh look, Rose, there is that duke we saw the last time," Laia said, trying to nudge her horse forward so that she could ride next to her sister.

"Yes—Lord Hawksmore," Rose said, giving a delicate nod of her head towards him. "But Laia, please do rein in. It wouldn't be right for you to abandon Thalia, and there isn't room for the four of us to ride abreast."

Laia gave a little pout and then fell behind again to ride next to her sister.

Rose turned and gave Lord Kirtland a smile. "I am sorry, my lord, I did not mean to push you aside."

"Quite all right. Hopefully, your sister will remember her manners this time and stay where she belongs."

Rose took a quick look at her new fiancé. Had he really meant the comment to sound so unkind? He had a bit of a smile on his face, however, so Rose assumed he had made a joke. She forced out a little giggle in response.

She looked around at the fashionable men and women of the *haute ton* who were riding through the park. Did they know? Did they know that she and Lord Kirtland were engaged? It was probably much too soon for anyone to have learned about it, but deep in her heart, she wished they had.

She was so happy that Lord Kirtland had finally proposed to her that she just wanted to shout it out—well, perhaps that was too strong, but she was certainly quite thrilled with her new state.

She was also quite desperate for her sisters to make a good impression on Lord Kirtland, and vice-versa. But so far, that had proved impossible with the way they were riding. Perhaps she could figure out a way for her to switch places with Laia, and then with Thalia, so that her sisters could speak with her new fiancé.

"Do you think, Miss Grace, that you might be interested in viewing a private collection of antiquities?" Lord Kirtland asked, pulling her attention back to himself.

"I would indeed," Rose answered without hesitation.

"Excellent. I have recently had the honor of meeting Sir John Soane, and he invited me to view what he calls his 'Academy of Architecture.' I believe he has some very fine pieces from both Egypt and Greece on display."

"That sounds . . ."

"Oh Rose, look, there is Fungy!" Thalia cried loudly.

Rose turned around in her saddle. "Please, Thalia! Lower your voice. I am very happy you have spotted our good friend, but you must not shout so loud that everyone in the vicinity is aware of it as well," she said with much more severity than she had intended.

She turned back and stole a look at Lord Kirtland to see how he had reacted, and was a little disturbed to see that he was looking approvingly at her. She gave him a little smile and asked, "Would you mind, sir, if we stopped for a moment to speak with him?"

"No, not at all."

It turned out that she need not have asked, for the gentleman himself had spotted them and was riding over to greet them. He was accompanied by Lady Mirthwood, riding a dappled gray mare.

Were the two of them inseparable? Rose's thought was accompanied by a flash of anger. She immediately quelled the feeling, reprimanding herself sternly and giving them both her brightest smile.

Fungy was mounted on a fine black gelding with a white blaze on his nose. And as always, he was dressed impeccably.

"Oh, Fungy, what an exceedingly fine horse," Thalia exclaimed as he got closer.

Fungy gave a little bow. "Why, thank you, Miss Thalia. I have heard that you were a very fine judge of horseflesh."

The girl beamed happily.

"How do you do, Lady Mirthwood? It is good to see you again," Rose said, doing her best to be polite and kind. If Fungy was close to the woman, then the very least Rose could do was to be courteous.

"You are looking very well today, Miss Grace. You have a very becoming blush to your cheeks," Lady Mirthwood said.

"Oh!" Rose put a hand to her cheeks, but couldn't imagine why they were flushed. Perhaps her happiness with the day? Or with her engagement? Her happiness in seeing Fungy again—and Lady Mirthwood, of course, she added. Why, it could be so many different reasons.

"It is probably the heat, that is all," she said, laughing off her sudden embarrassment.

Rose was thrilled when Fungy managed to position

his horse between her and Lord Kirtland, for she particularly wanted a private word with him.

She leaned forward in order to speak more softly to him while Lady Mirthwood and Lord Kirtland exchanged pleasantries.

"Fungy, I just cannot thank you enough for what you did yesterday. I really do not deserve such a good friend as you have shown yourself to be."

"Just seeing you happy is all the thanks that I need. And what happened to you calling me by my given name?" he teased.

He spoke just as quietly as she had, but somehow he made it seem so intimate and exciting. His deep, rich voice sent tingles through Rose, warming her in odd places.

She gave a little embarrassed laugh. "I do apologize. You have been so good to me, Sinjin. Indeed, I do feel that we are close enough friends now so that I may address you by your given name. I promise to do so from now on."

"Miss Grace, your sisters are an abomination!" Lord Kirtland's voice interrupted, dispelling all of her good feelings.

"I beg your pardon?" she said, straightening her back and turning to him. She desperately hoped that she had misheard him.

"Just look at them, galloping off like . . . like hoydens. It is beyond words how rude and inappropriate their behavior is—in the park, at the height of the promenade!"

Her heart leapt into her throat. She turned to Sinjin, but he had already turned his horse around and was about to set off after her wayward sisters. "Have no fear, Rose, I will see that they come to no harm, nor accidentally cause any."

Immediately she felt relieved, knowing that he would

take care of everything. "Thank you, Sinjin. I knew I could count on you," she said quickly, as he rode off.

Still, she could not help but be worried. The park was so crowded today that the galloping of Thalia and Laia's horses through the crowded bridle paths was sure to startle a number of other horses, if not worse. She sincerely hoped that no one would be injured.

"My goodness, are your sisters always so daring?" Lady Mirthwood asked.

"Daring is not the word I would use, my lady. Disobedient would be my guess. Either that, or so poorly raised that they know no better," Lord Kirtland said angrily. "And after their behavior so far today, I would assume the latter."

Rose opened her mouth to protest his harsh words, but then remembered that she was engaged to be married to this man. She should not argue with him. When they were married, what he said would be law.

But just as quickly as this thought entered Rose's mind, she threw it right back out again. This was no time to be timid and ladylike. These were her sisters he had just insulted!

"How dare you, Lord Kirtland!" she said, allowing her anger full rein. "My sisters and I may have been raised in an unconventional manner, but that is only to be expected in a foreign country and on an expedition. My parents did the best they could under the circumstance, and I think they did an exceptional job."

She paused to still her suddenly shifting horse, which was clearly feeling her excitement and anger.

"If Laia and Thalia do not always behave just as they should, then perhaps it is my fault for being too lenient with them. I am the one who has been in charge of them since my mother's death over a year ago, and indeed for much of their lives."

"A child bringing up other children? No wonder they are so ignorant," Lord Kirtland sneered.

"I am no child, sir, and I am doing the best I can," Rose said, defending herself.

"Miss Laia and Thalia *are* still children, my lord. You must remember that, and not be so harsh on them," Lady Mirthwood said, coming to Rose's aid, for which she was very grateful.

Lord Kirtland raised his eyebrows and then turned back to Rose. "How old are your sisters, Miss Grace?"

"Thalia is fifteen and Laia seventeen."

He gave Lady Mirthwood a smug look. "They are not children, Lady Mirthwood. They are old enough to know better." He turned back to Rose. "And I assure you, when they are under my care, I will *not* be so lenient as you have clearly been, no matter where in the world we are."

Rose could not respond due to Sinjin's return with the two girls.

"Oh, Sinjin, I cannot thank you enough! Girls, what have you to say for yourselves?" Rose said, spurring her horse forward while looking severely at her sisters.

They were both looking very flushed as well as a little repentant, but both still had that twinkle of mischief in their eyes.

"We have already had a word," Sinjin said.

"Well, I think that they deserve more than just a word! A good beating would be more like . . ." Lord Kirtland began.

"My lord! Thank you very much, but I will deal with my sisters as I see fit," Rose said, sternly.

"Oh, no! They were just having a bit of a lark," Sinjin said. "No harm done—to them or to anyone else. And I'm certain they won't do it again. Will you, ladies?"

The two girls covered up their giggles, but shook their heads.

Rose gave them a little smile, and to Sinjin as well. He had clearly done an excellent job of informing them of their mistake in such a way that they would neither repeat it, nor feel so rebellious that they would go out and cause more trouble. Firm but gentle—that was the way to deal with Laia and Thalia, as Rose knew.

"I believe it is time we headed for home, my lord," Rose said to Lord Kirtland.

"Indeed, perhaps well past."

She turned back to Sinjin and Lady Mirthwood. "I am so sorry for the trouble we caused. It was wonderful to see you again."

"No problem at all," they said, as they waved them off.

Lord Kirtland led Rose and her sisters out the nearest gate and then back towards their home.

As they trotted sedately down the lane, Rose felt that she should try and make amends with her fiancé. Perhaps he would understand if she just explained the situation to him.

"My lord, you must not be so angry with the girls. They were clearly itching for a little fun after having to ride so sedately around the park with little amusement," she said.

Lord Kirtland turned to her, his face still a little pinched with annoyance. "Miss Grace, girls the ages of your sisters should know to behave better. Indeed, they should count themselves lucky to have so much as a sedate walk in the park, especially at the height of the promenade."

To Rose's dismay, his voice became implacable. "No, I must reiterate—when they are under my control, such behavior will not only not be tolerated, but punished appropriately."

Rose quickly turned to look behind her at her sisters, giving them a silent, imploring look to not speak a word of what she was sure they were thinking. Fortunately, they understood, and kept quiet until they had said good-bye to Lord Kirtland and seen their horses taken away to the stable.

But once inside their own drawing room, they let loose.

"Rose, how *could* you not defend us?"

"He is the most *horrendous* man I ever hope to meet!"

"You cannot mean to actually marry him!"

"Oh no, Rose, you cannot. Papa could not force you to do so, could he?"

Rose held up her hands to stem the flow of their words.

"I *did* defend you, Laia! I did so quite strongly while Sinjin, er, Fungy was off rescuing you from your own folly. Even Lady Mirthwood put in a word in your defense. But I must say that what you did was truly indefensible. You know that running off pell-mell like that could have hurt someone or yourselves."

She stopped to take a breath and shake her head reprovingly. But unbidden, a smile forced its way onto her lips. That was quickly followed by a giggle, which she quickly hid behind her hand.

But it was no use. Before she knew it, she was working hard to contain her laughter.

Her sisters joined her immediately, and soon the three girls were laughing hysterically.

When Rose finally caught her breath, she said, "It was really too bad of you. But goodness, I cannot blame you at all. A more staid and boring outing and with so little to amuse yourselves . . . Even I was itching for a good gallop!"

"Oh, Rose." Thalia jumped up and threw her arms around her sister's neck. "I am so happy that you are still you!"

"Why, whatever do you mean, Thalia?"

"It is just that I thought you would become stiff

and stuffy like Lord Kirtland now that you are engaged to him."

"Really, Rose, you cannot marry that man. He is awful!"

Rose felt very worried. Her sisters were right. How could she marry a man who had absolutely no sense of humor at all? Stiff and stuffy described him perfectly.

But did she really have a choice?

With an ache forming in her chest, she shook her head. "I *have* to marry him. He is rich, and will solve all of our financial problems. He will pay our debts, and in a few years I'll be able to sponsor Laia for her come-out. I really don't have an option."

The sad looks on her sisters' faces said it all. And it was just how she felt as well, now that she was beginning to know Lord Kirtland better.

There was one truth that this day's outing had taught her—Lord Kirtland was certainly not going to be the knight in shining armor she had always fantasized about as a child.

"Don't worry. He's really not *that* bad. And remember, he is an archeologist," she told her sisters, trying to shed some positive light on what was looking more and more like a dreadful mistake.

# 23

By the following Monday, when Lord Kirtland picked up Rose to take her to Sir John Soane's Academy of Architecture, enough time had passed so that she could distance herself from the events of that fateful ride in the park, and look at what had occurred rationally. She still did not blame her sisters for their behavior, but was no longer quite so upset by Lord Kirtland's reaction.

The still outstanding bills, however, were strongly weighing on her mind. She had received notes once again from both the mantua maker and cloth merchant, reminding her of the money she owed. To make things worse, she still could not rid her mind of the debt she owed to Lord Kirtland himself.

There had to be something she could do to dispel these debts. And she wasn't sure that she could wait six months or a year until she was wed to do so.

No, she decided, it was time to come clean to Lord Kirtland. Oh, she wouldn't tell him about the bills just yet, but perhaps she could speak to him about her gambling debts.

Surely he would forgive her the money she owed

to him now that they were engaged to be married? Without a doubt, she had to ask.

With this in mind, she found herself unable to fully concentrate on the wonders of Sir John's magnificent collection. This disturbed her, but until she spoke with Lord Kirtland there was nothing she could do.

At the first opportunity, she broached the subject delicately. "My lord, there is a favor I was wondering if I might ask of you."

Lord Kirtland looked from a striking collection of Greek vases to her with a look of mild surprise. "What might that be?"

"It is concerning the vowel you wrote for me, to Mr. Aiken," she began.

"Oh? I will be happy to escort you to Lady Kemble's card party tomorrow night, so that you can try once again to win the money back," he offered.

"Thank you, but I was wondering, actually, if you might forgive the debt altogether?" she said quickly.

Lord Kirtland turned toward Rose rather swiftly. "What do you mean? I paid your debt for you, and now you want me to just forget it?"

"Well . . ." Rose swallowed hard.

"Miss Grace, are you suggesting that you wish to go back on your word?" Lord Kirtland asked, drawing down his eyebrows in a vicious way.

"I . . ."

"I paid your debt for you because I thought that you were honest. I trusted you." He turned around to look back at the vase for a moment and then turned back to Rose. "That you would think so little of your own honor is appalling, Miss Grace."

"It is not that! I always do my utmost to hold to my word. In fact, I do not believe I have ever gone back on it," Rose said, horrified that he would think so little of her.

"Well, then, I trust that you *will* repay this debt."

"I . . . I cannot." The words came out as a whisper. She just could not say them outright.

Lord Kirtland froze at her words. A little smile, although not a very pleasant one, crept onto his face. "You surely do not mean that you cannot. You mean that you do not have the funds just at this moment. I understand, Miss Grace. Your father has been away and you have not yet received your pin money this quarter."

He turned and took a few steps away. With a nonchalant wave of his hand, he continued, "That is perfectly fine. I have no problems waiting until your father returns from his estate. You may pay me when it is convenient. And because we are engaged to be married, I shall not even charge you any interest on the loan."

"But . . ."

"No. No need to thank me, Miss Grace. It is perfectly all right." He gave her another fleeting smile. "Of course, it is entirely possible that you shall win it all back tomorrow night and none of this will have been necessary at all."

He then turned away from her once again to move on to the next exhibit. Rose followed him in silence. There did not seem to be any way out, short of telling Lord Kirtland outright that neither she nor her father had the money to pay this debt. It didn't seem right to try and win it back either, especially since she no longer had any money with which to gamble.

"No. I thank you, my lord. I do not believe I shall be attending Lady Kemble's card party tomorrow night. I will find another way to pay you back, and as quickly as possible," Rose said finally when they stopped to look at some statuettes. She turned back to the exhibit, but still could find no amusement in it.

It turned out to be a very bleak afternoon.

After reaching home, she explained all that had

happened to her sisters. "But I just don't know what to do. I could not tell him that we didn't have the money." She paused. "Papa will be incredibly angry when he finds out what I have done, and rightfully so."

Thalia and Laia just looked at each other. Clearly, they were at a loss as well. Thalia, always the optimist, said, "Don't worry, Rose, we'll figure *something* out."

"Yes, and after we do, you won't have to marry that horrid man after all," Laia added.

Rose smiled at her sisters, but could not imagine that they would be able to come up with anything either.

"Where is Laia?" Aunt Farmington asked the following evening, as she, Thalia, and Rose sat in the drawing room enjoying a quiet evening at home.

"She has gone to bed early. She wasn't feeling very well," Thalia answered, hardly pausing in her practicing of the pianoforte.

"Really, I was not aware of this," Rose said with real concern—Laia never got ill.

Thalia got a scared look in her eye for a moment, and then immediately focused her eyes downward to her fingers. "Oh yes, well, it is just a headache, I believe. I am sure she will be absolutely fine tomorrow."

"Well, that is a relief. I am certain I would not know what to do with a sick child," Aunt Farmington said.

Rose could not be fooled so easily, however. Not by either of her sisters. She set aside her sewing. "I think I will just take a peek in on her then, just to make sure everything is all right."

Thalia jumped up. "Oh, no, Rose, you needn't do that. I shall go up if you like."

Now she was certain that her sisters were up to something. "That is very kind of you, Thalia, but no, I'll go myself."

She walked quickly up to the room shared by her two younger sisters, Thalia following anxiously on her heels. As she expected, the room was empty. She went in anyway, and then turned toward her youngest sister as soon as the door was closed.

"Where is she? And what are you two up to?"

Thalia was a little taken aback by the sudden attack. However, she recovered herself quickly. "She is just out doing what you refused to do," she said, crossing her arms defiantly.

"What do you mean?"

"I mean, she is out trying to win back the money you lost."

"But . . . but she doesn't even know how to play whist!"

"Yes she does. We found a book at the lending library explaining exactly how to play, and even explaining some tricks on how to win," Thalia said, quite thrilled with herself.

Rose opened her mouth, but could not manage to put all of the thousands of thoughts and fears that were running through her mind into a coherent sentence.

How could her sister be so stupid as to put herself at risk with such an outrageous scheme? With what money was she playing? How did she get to the party? And what if someone recognized her?

On and on the questions went, increasing her worry with every passing moment. There was only one thing to do, she realized with a moan of chagrin—she had to go and save her!

Without a further word to her sister, she ran to her own room and went to her armoire for her domino and mask. Of course, they were gone. Laia had taken them!

"Rose, what are you going to do?" Thalia asked. She had followed Rose into her room.

"I am going to fetch her, only . . ."

Rose paced back and forth in her room. What was

she to do? She could not go to a card party without some sort of mask to hide behind.

"Only what?"

"Laia took my domino and mask. I cannot go without them."

Then she remembered that she had an old cloak that had once belonged to her mother. It was quite tattered, but that hardly mattered just now. At least it had a large hood which she could use to hide herself. It would have to do.

It took Rose and Thalia a good ten or fifteen minutes to find it—time that she did not have to waste. The sooner she got to the card party, the sooner she could rescue Laia from the lure of the cards, and probably the less money they would owe.

"Make sure Aunt Farmington does not notice anything is amiss. I am counting on you," she whispered to her sister just before she slipped out the back door.

# 24

Sinjin drained the wine from his glass and then, without hesitation, immediately filled it up again. There was something soothing in the wine, although the alcohol had not yet begun to affect him. He would need another few glasses, he supposed, just to get him through another evening of appearing as if everything was normal.

Each day, it was becoming more and more difficult to assume his usual practiced ennui. He was actually surprised at how easy it was to revert back to his old self—and how comfortable it felt behaving that way.

But he could not do so tonight. Tonight, it was the old Fungy who needed to make an appearance, and Sinjin would have to be suppressed once more.

With a sigh and another fortifying sip, he turned to see the clothes his valet had been carefully laying out for him to wear this evening.

"Thomas, what is this? How long have you been in my employ that you cannot put together a simple suit of clothes for me to wear?" he snapped, suddenly feeling a burning rage in the pit of his stomach, in addition to the pounding headache that had become his constant companion over the past few days. Something so simple, so utterly simple, and the man just could not manage it?

His valet looked down at the black pantaloons, which he had coupled with a dark green coat and a waistcoat with green and gold embroidery. "I beg your pardon, sir," he said, but then hesitated over which piece of the offending suit to remove.

Sinjin gave him a minute to figure out what he had done wrong, but clearly the man was completely incapable. With another burst of anger, he picked up the coat and tossed it at him. "Take out my black coat if you are having me wear black pantaloons, man."

"Yes, sir," Thomas said, hastening to do his master's bidding.

Immediately, Sinjin felt a stab of remorse shooting through him. He dropped back down into the chair in front of his dressing table, sighing and rubbing at his forehead. "I am sorry, Thomas. Didn't mean to snap at you like that. Not your fault."

"If I may say so, sir, you have not been quite yourself the past few days," Thomas offered gently.

"No, I have not been sleeping well at all," Sinjin said, inspecting his reflection in his shaving mirror. The bags under his eyes had grown into pouches, and his usually sparkling eyes looked back at him rather dully.

Losing Rose to Kirtland had been more difficult than he could have possibly imagined. Then having Georgiana turn him down as well had completely destroyed any ideas he had had of marrying and starting a family.

Dreams of drowning still haunted his nights. And although he awoke each morning determined to live up to his own resolutions, with each day those resolutions seemed harder and harder to attain.

At least he still had Lord Halsbury and his assignment—although he didn't know how much closer he was to coming to a conclusion on that front either. Perhaps if he made a list of possible suspects . . .

Sinjin abandoned his valet and strode to the drawing room and his writing table, determined to at least have something tangible to show Lord Halsbury the next time they met.

Sitting down, he pulled out a piece of paper and a pen, and opened his ink stand.

Who were the people he had watched so far? What had he to go on?

He pulled out his penknife. Slowly and carefully, he began sharpening his quill as he thought. *P.H., P.H.*— he could still think of only Lord Pemberton-Howe and Pip Haston among society members with those initials. He dipped his pen into the ink, and jotted down the first of the names on his paper.

Immediately, he crossed it off. It couldn't be Pemberton-Howe—he had been out of town for the past week, and in that time Cole had lost nearly a thousand pounds. He also simply could not imagine Rose's rather unworldly father as the leader of a gambling scheme.

That left just Pip Haston. Sinjin was about to begin writing the name when he was interrupted by a knock on the door.

"Fungy! Still not dressed?" Julian said, strolling into the room.

"Ah, no. Sorry, just finishing something up."

Silently, he cursed his good friend for being so timely, and himself for having forgotten that he had invited him to accompany him out.

He turned back to his paper, but felt Julian's presence right behind him. He was looking over his shoulder.

Sinjin could not let his friend know what he was up to—it would give rise to too many questions he did not want to answer. Quickly, he switched to spelling out Haston's name phonetically in Greek, mentally thanking Rose for inspiring him to begin reading Greek again.

There was one other name he had meant to write . . . yes, Kirtland. He started to think of the k sound in Greek, but then remembered that Kirtland was the man's title. What was his name? Ah, Roland Egerton. That was easy enough.

A thrill of excitement and remembrance of his youth sung through his veins as he wrote out the name phonetically in Greek. He still had it. He had not completely forgotten everything—amazing how a language could come back so quickly after so many years.

Finally, he stood up and greeted Julian properly.

"Welcome, old man. Sorry about that," he said.

"Not a problem. Amazing how you can just write in, what is that, Greek? Just like that. Although, I suppose it is not too different from me being able to write in Bengali. But still, your scribbles *are* all Greek to me," Julian said, laughing at his own joke.

Sinjin laughed too, determined to be merry, despite his earlier bout of moroseness. But when he turned back momentarily to the list he had made, he suddenly felt as if he had had all the wind knocked out of him.

There it was, clearly written in his own neat hand, Roland Egerton in Greek—*Ρολανδ Ηγηρτον*.

P.H.

Sinjin staggered back a step.

"Fungy, are you all right?" Julian grabbed Sinjin's arm to support him.

Sinjin took a step forward to balance himself and turned to look Julian in the eye.

"Of course! The man is an archeologist. What an idiot I am not to have thought of this. He certainly reads Greek, wouldn't be surprised if he even wrote in it occasionally. And if signing a note . . . he wouldn't use his English initials . . ."

"What on earth are you talking about?" Julian asked, completely confused.

Sinjin laughed with overwhelming relief and gave Julian a big bear hug. He then ran to his room to get dressed. Calling back over his shoulder, he shouted, "I'm a genius, Julian! Just be happy to know that you are friends with an absolute genius!"

Julian laughed. "I always knew that, Fungy. I just wished I could follow what you were saying." Julian came into Sinjin's room as he was just finishing buttoning his pantaloons.

"No need, my friend." And indeed, he would not want him to. It would spoil his entire investigation, he thought to himself as he tied his neckcloth. Now, he only needed to catch that rascal Kirtland at his own game.

When his neckcloth was tied perfectly, he asked, "Where were we supposed to go this evening?"

"To Lady Baskin's soiree."

"Ah right. Mind if we go to Lady Kemble's card party instead?"

"Not terribly. Is there a reason why you would rather go there?"

"Yes. Isn't it obvious?" Sinjin laughed.

"Fungy." Julian put his hand on his friend's shoulder as he was buttoning his waistcoat. "I heard from Merry and Sin that they had met you at a gambling hell the other night. Is there a problem? I've got plenty of the ready, if you're in need."

Sinjin stopped dressing. "What?" He then burst out laughing. "Oh no, Julian. No. Thank you. You are a good friend."

"But Fungy . . . a gambling hell, and now a card party? If you are not in debt, then why this sudden interest?"

"It is . . . er, well, I'm afraid you will just have to wait to find out. I'm sorry, Julian, truly I am, but I can't tell you just now," Sinjin said.

How he wished that he could tell him. Perhaps he

would have even been able to enlist his aid in catching Lord Kirtland. But he just could not. Not without speaking to Lord Halsbury about it first.

And besides, he did so want to be the one who caught him. It really did have to be entirely his work that brought Kirtland to justice. A wonderful chill of excitement and anticipation ran through him.

"You will just have to trust me. I am not in debt or in any sort of trouble, I assure you. You will learn it all before too long, if my suspicions are correct."

He grabbed his coat and put it on as he headed out the door. "Come along now, I can't afford to be late," he said, as if it were Julian who had been the one taking up time.

Julian chuckled bemusedly as he followed him out the door.

# 25

Sinjin walked into Lady Kemble's with Julian hard on his heels. Perhaps, he thought, still glowing with excitement, his friend assumed that sticking close to him was the way to get to the bottom of all of his elusiveness.

However, all it did was to make him bump right into Sinjin when he stopped short just inside the door to the drawing room.

Quite a few eyes were trained on two remarkably dressed ladies. The first was in a deep red domino, the second in a faded, rather shabby blue cloak. They were standing on the far side of the room having an argument, albeit a whispered one. The lady in blue even went so far as to try and grab the arm of the lady in red and pull her away.

A flash of gold on her wrist had Sinjin rushing to the scene. He knew that bracelet. And Fungy could never allow Miss Grace to embarrass herself in public, it just wasn't done.

"Good evening, ladies," he said smoothly, but quietly, approaching them just before their hostess did. "I believe it would be best if you took your argument outside."

He then turned to Lady Kemble. "Do not worry,

ma'am, I will ensure that there will be no further
disruption to your party."

Lady Kemble looked very relieved. She clearly had
not relished the thought of having to deal with this
altercation herself. "Oh, thank you, Fungy, I always
know that I can count on you."

Sinjin gave her a little bow, and then firmly took
each lady by her elbow and led them both out onto
the terrace. Julian followed closely behind.

Sinjin's job had just gotten much more difficult. He
hadn't expected to find Rose here this evening and
hadn't even considered the social ramifications Kirtland's downfall would have on her.

Naturally, once it was known throughout the *ton* that
Kirtland was a crook, everyone would look askance
at Rose, wondering if she had been an accomplice or
just another innocent who had been duped by him.
Either way, her reputation would end up in tatters.

As soon as they were out of sight of the rest of the
party, Rose threw back her hood. "Thank you, Sinjin.
I was attempting to get my sister out of there, but she
would not listen."

Laia, too, threw back her hood and mask, revealing her distinctive bright red hair. "I can't believe that
you would want me to leave when I was finally winning
back the money that *you* lost!"

"It doesn't matter what you were doing. You should
not have been there in the first place!" Rose said
emphatically.

Sinjin immediately could see that both ladies were
much too upset to get any further in their argument.
They both clearly needed a minute to calm down, so
he provided a diversion.

"Miss Laia, may I present my good friend, the Earl
of Huntley?"

Both girls stopped glaring at each other to ob-
serve the social niceties and greet Julian.

Julian bowed over Laia's hand, using his usual pleasant and open charm to defuse the tension, as Sinjin knew he would. "It is very nice to meet you, Miss Laia. May I ask how you managed to get into the party? I assume you were not invited."

Laia gave a guilty little smile. "It was quite easy, actually, my lord. The back gate to the garden was open, so I just slipped in."

"You just stole into a stranger's garden?" Rose was aghast.

"What if you had gone through the wrong gate?" Julian asked.

"I counted the number of houses from the front, and then the number of garden doors in the back. And I figured if I had gotten the wrong one, I could just slip away again," Laia explained with a little shrug of her shoulders.

"That was extremely bold of you," Sinjin said, "but now you must make your exit and do so as unobtrusively as possible. But through the front door this time."

"But I don't want to leave!" Laia protested.

"It doesn't matter what you want right now, Laia, that is the right thing to do," her sister said gently.

"I am afraid you must always do the right thing, no matter how boring that is, Miss Laia, just as we discussed in the park the other day," Sinjin said, hoping that his influence would help to convince the girl, who had the look of a stubborn child just now.

"But I was winning!" Laia argued.

Winning? From Kirtland? Sinjin wondered what his game was, and how deeply involved Rose was.

"That's wonderful, Laia, but you should not have been here in the first place. A seventeen-year-old girl cannot be allowed to attend, nor gamble, at a card party," Rose said with finality.

"Afraid she's right, Miss Laia. It is not strictly proper

for even Rose to come to such things," Sinjin said, still holding out hope that she could be convinced to leave quietly.

"She did so once before." Laia pouted.

"Yes, but she was here both in a domino and escorted by a gentleman. The rules could be bent a little."

More and more, Sinjin was wishing that Rose had never become entangled with Kirtland. The only way for her to come out of Kirtland's unmasking unscathed was for her to distance herself from him right away. Sinjin just wasn't sure how he was going to convince her to do so without jeopardizing his entire investigation, or their friendship.

"Well, I am here in a domino," Laia said.

"But you should not be here at all," Sinjin explained, beginning to lose his patience.

"I would be happy to escort you home, Miss Laia," Julian offered.

Sinjin was now very grateful for his presence. He would end up being useful after all.

"Thank you, my lord, that is very kind of you," Rose said, accepting his offer without hesitation.

"But what about my game? I was winning," Laia complained, now beginning to sound more like the child she still was.

"Your game is over, Laia," Rose said.

Julian nodded, but then raised one finger and said, "However, if one of you doesn't go back in to continue her game, won't it be obvious what has happened?" Julian asked.

"Not only that, but I've only won forty pounds," Laia said, trying another tack to get her sister's permission to return to her game. "You still owe another sixty that you can't pay. I've got to go back and try to win that money, Rose."

"No, you don't!" Rose and Sinjin said simultaneously. Sinjin could not allow either Laia or her sister to go back to gambling with Lord Kirtland. If they had only lost one hundred pounds, they had been lucky so far. But he could not allow them to risk any more money—and now it was clear that this was money they didn't have.

"But . . ."

"No, Laia. I told you, gambling is not the way to pay that debt," Rose said.

"Please listen to your sister, Miss Laia. If you continue to gamble with Lord Kirtland, you will only get further and further into debt," Sinjin said.

Laia looked from her sister to Sinjin, clearly at a loss. "But I was winning."

"I assure you, it wouldn't have continued," Sinjin said as gently as he could.

"You don't know that," Laia said, crossing her arms in front of her.

"Yes, I do." Sinjin stopped. He could not tell them what he had learned about Lord Kirtland.

But how could he not?

This assignment was becoming more onerous by the moment.

But first things first. Laia *had* to go home.

"Julian, I think now would be an excellent time for you to escort Miss Laia home."

Julian bowed to the young lady, who was still very reluctant to go.

"Please, Miss Laia," Julian said very gently but firmly, while holding out his arm for her to take.

With a pout, she put her hood and mask back on. Taking his arm, she allowed him to escort her back into the house and from there, home.

Rose turned to Sinjin as soon as her sister was gone. "I don't know how to thank you, Sinjin . . ."

"You won't thank me once you hear what I need to tell you."

He still couldn't figure out why Kirtland had involved Rose in the first place. Why had he targeted her? She was not an heiress.

"What is it? Do you think that Laia's reputation has already been destroyed by this? As long as no one finds out it was she . . ."

"No. It is not that. This concerns Lord Kirtland." Sinjin took a deep breath. "Can you think of any reason why Lord Kirtland would want to win money from you, Rose?" Sinjin asked, delaying the inevitable.

Rose paused, looking very confused. She shook her head slowly. "He has not won money from me, it was Mr. Aiken to whom I lost. Lord Kirtland was kind enough to write a vowel to him for me which is how I came to owe the money to him instead."

Sinjin nodded. "Yes, but there still has to be a reason why he wanted you indebted to him."

And then it hit him. "Ah! It isn't you he wants under his thumb, it must be Lord Pemberton-Howe."

"What? What are you . . ."

Sinjin looked at Rose intently. "Kirtland is an archeologist. He probably needs your father's name to lend credit to his own archeological aspirations."

"Well, of course, he will receive any help he needs from my father. We are to be married."

"But you should not."

"But . . . What do you mean? I thought you were happy for me. It was you who made it possible."

"I know, I am, well, I was happy for you."

"And now?"

"Now I have learned something that makes it impossible for you to marry him." Sinjin took a deep breath and braced himself for any possible response— it was unlikely that she was going to take this with any sort of equanimity. "Rose, I am sorry, but Lord Kirtland has been stealing people's money through gambling."

"Gambling is not stealing!" Rose scoffed. "If people gambled and lost to him, there is nothing wrong with that. I am not particularly happy that I lost money to Mr. Aiken, but it was my own fault."

"No, it wasn't. I am certain that Kirtland and Aiken are working together. Together they are cheating people out of their money."

Rose gasped. "Do you have proof?"

"No, but . . ."

"Sinjin, I don't know why you would stoop to making unfounded accusations."

"I am not . . ."

"No? Then what do you call accusing Lord Kirtland of the most heinous crime, without being able to back up your suppositions. Why this sudden hatred of him?"

Rose held up her hand as Sinjin began to try to explain himself. "No, do not answer. Nothing you can say could convince me that what you are saying is the truth. You have no proof, and if you tell me anything more, it will only convince me that you are making this up out of whole cloth."

"But, Rose . . ."

"No, Sinjin. I am very sorry. I am sorry that you are so troubled by my happiness that you would . . . would lie to me. I had thought . . . well, that is no matter," Rose wiped her hand along her cheek. Was there a tear?

She shook her head and continued. "Sinjin, you have been a very good friend to me. This pains me a great deal, but since you cannot seem to come to terms with the fact that I am happily engaged to marry another man, I think it would be better if you and I did not see or speak to one another anymore. I thank you for your assistance this evening. Good night."

And with that, she turned and went back into the drawing room, pulling up her hood as she did so.

He had failed. He had tried to save her, but this time she had not let him.

A well of pain opened up in the pit of his stomach.

When it was vital that he convince her to end her engagement and disassociate herself from this crook, all he had succeeded in doing was ending their friendship—something that meant more to him than nearly anything else in this world.

She hadn't even listened to him, but had immediately jumped to the conclusion that he was jealous. What hurt most was that it was true, he *had* been jealous. He could not deny that.

But now . . . He swallowed hard at the taste of bile that burned at the back of his mouth. Now he had to put aside his personal feelings. He had a job to do, and there was no way out of it. He had taken on the responsibility and he would carry it out.

He took a step inside the drawing room and saw Rose speaking quietly with Lady Kemble. Probably making excuses for her sister having to leave.

With a sigh, he turned to watch Lord Kirtland. He was playing with Jack Abbey, another on the list of potential victims.

There was nothing more he could do. He had to go immediately to Lord Halsbury and report what he had learned. Hopefully, Kirtland would be stopped quickly, and Rose would bear no more than a little humiliation from having been associated with him.

She didn't ever want to see or speak with him again.

He had known the consequence and yet he had had to go through with it anyway. Why? Why had he set himself up for such a great fall?

No, there was no use in asking himself that. He knew the answer. And yet, once again, Sinjin felt as if his heart had been trampled upon—only this time his much abused organ was too numb to feel any pain.

As he slowly meandered out of the house, he wondered how many times a man's heart could be broken before it just gave out on him altogether.

# 26

Rose sat stitching quietly in the corner of the drawing room. Every so often a tear would fall, unbidden, onto her work. She did not try to stop them. It was futile.

After the events of last night, both of her sisters had left her alone for a while that morning. She was certain that Laia was still upset that she had been forced to leave the party. And it was likely that she had told Thalia everything, including how unfair she and Sinjin had been to her.

But they did not know what had occurred after Laia had left.

How could Sinjin have been so cruel to her last night? Didn't he realize that Lord Kirtland was the only person who could save her family from financial ruin? And to accuse him of cheating! Of stealing money. It could not be true.

No, the only reason Sinjin had done this must be because he was jealous. She had thought that he'd been happy for her. He had seemed fine the other day when they had met in the park. She just could not imagine what had happened between then and last night. What had made him change his mind about accepting her engagement to Lord Kirtland?

Rose put down her embroidery to blow her nose.

She jumped as the drawing room door abruptly flew open, banging against the adjacent wall.

"My dear . . ." Aunt Farmington nearly ran into the room and then stopped short. She scanned the room and then found Rose in the corner.

"Oh, my dear Rose, you simply would not believe what I have heard!" she exclaimed, walking briskly toward her. Rose had never seen her move so quickly. Surely there was something seriously wrong.

Rose stood up. "What is it, Aunt? What has happened?"

Thalia and Laia had also jumped up at their aunt's dramatic entrance.

"Is it Papa? Has something happened to him?" Thalia cried.

Aunt Farmington turned on the girl. "Your Papa? No, why, have you heard something?"

"No, only you seem to be very upset about some news. I thought it might be . . ."

"Oh, no. It is Lord Kirtland," she said, turning back to Rose.

"Lord Kirtland? What about him?"

"He and Mr. Aiken have fled the country! Everyone is talking about it! Apparently the two of them have been working together to cheat at cards. They were caught last night at Lady Kemble's card party by . . ." she paused dramatically. "You will never guess!"

"Fungy," Rose whispered.

Aunt Farmington suddenly deflated. "Yes! How did you know?"

"He mentioned something to me the last time I saw him," she said. She knew her voice sounded hollow, but she simply could not gather up the emotional energy to put any life into it.

She dropped back down into her chair.

"Oh my dear, I am so glad that you were not present. It would have been beyond humiliating. Well, as it is, nearly everyone knows that you were engaged to Lord Kirtland."

"They do?"

"Oh well, of course, my dear. We were all so happy that you'd made such a good match. Why, I must have told at least ten people and then, of course, they would have gone about telling people, and well, you know how it is."

She tsked sadly and shook her head. "Who would have known that such a pleasant gentleman would do such a thing? And we all thought he was wealthy! Why, he must have been as poor as a church mouse!"

"Not if he was cheating at cards," Thalia said. "That would have made him quite wealthy, I imagine."

"Oh, well, yes, of course," her aunt agreed.

"What are you going to do, Rose?" Laia asked.

Rose felt as if her head was in a thick fog. She could not focus her mind on the overwhelming news and its consequences. She looked up at her sister. "I don't know. I'm not sure there is anything I can do."

"Well, no, of course not. Your engagement is, naturally, at an end. Well, with the gentleman having fled the country," Aunt Farmington said, moving away to sit down on the sofa now that her news was told.

"Thalia, dear, ring for some tea," her aunt requested, now sounding very tired.

"That means that we no longer have a way to pay our bills," Thalia pointed out needlessly as she walked to the hearth to pull the bell cord.

"And there aren't any other wealthy gentlemen for Rose to marry," Laia added.

"Not only that, my dears, but no man would even consider becoming engaged to her now. Well, at least not for a good long time. The stigma, you know," Aunt

Farmington added, wiping delicately at the corners of her eyes. "And I am afraid it may rub off on Thalia and Laia as well. None of you will have an easy time of it, I fear."

With that bit of news, Rose completely lost hold of the tenuous control over her emotions that she had managed to maintain all morning. A shot of pure anguish racked her body, and her sisters rushed to her side as she let her sobs surge out.

"I have failed. I have failed you all," she said, when she could finally manage to speak.

"Oh, no, Rose. Not at all," Laia said, caressing her hair.

"You still have Fungy," Thalia offered.

Rose began to cry again, "No, I don't. When he told me that Lord Kirtland was cheating, I became angry and called him a liar. I . . . I told him that we should never see each other ever again."

"Oh dear," was all Laia could say.

"But why did you do something so stupid?" Thalia asked, bewildered.

Rose just shook her head and wiped at her tears with her soaking wet handkerchief. "I thought he was jealous or some such thing. I . . . I didn't want to believe that what he said was true. Lord Kirtland is all that we have . . . all that we *had* standing between us and the poorhouse, or, or debtor's prison. I don't . . . didn't *want* to marry him, I *had* to marry him. How could Sinjin not have known that? How could he have been so cruel as to take away my only hope!" Rose hit her leg with her fist, her tears turning to anger.

"I thought he loved you," Laia said, wiping away her own tears from her cheeks.

"He *is* horrible," Thalia agreed vehemently. "Some friend he turned out to be! Why I could . . ."

"No, Thalia," Laia interrupted her.

"Violence is never the answer, Thalia. I just don't

know what the answer may be," Rose said, trying to hold back a fresh wave of tears and failing miserably.

And it was into this melancholy scene that Lord Pemberton-Howe walked, not ten minutes later.

"My girls! My three beautiful graces, what has happened?" their father cried as soon as he had walked in the door and had taken stock of the room.

"Oh, Papa!" the girls said in unison.

Rose stood back and wiped her eyes with her soggy handkerchief, letting Thalia and Laia run and wrap their father in a dual hug.

"My dear, dear girls. I have missed you," he said, holding on to his two youngest daughters. "And my sweet Rosebud, why do you cry?" He caressed his eldest daughter's face, wiping away stray tears. "Has someone died? Aunt Farmington, you are well?"

"Oh, Papa," Rose said before her aunt could answer him. "It is . . . it is just that I have failed you," she said, trying to hold back her tears.

"How could you have possibly failed me, my love? What has happened?"

"You told me to marry quickly . . ." Rose began.

"And she almost did," Laia interrupted.

"But then he was found to be a cheater . . ." Thalia said, taking up the strain.

"And now he has fled the country," Laia ended.

"And she told Fungy never to see her again," Thalia added.

"So now we are completely in the suds," Laia finished, on the verge of tears herself.

Lord Pemberton-Howe tried to make sense of his daughter's disjointed tale. "Who was it that your sister nearly married?"

"Lord Kirtland," Thalia and Laia said in unison.

"Ah. The wealthy gentleman we met playing cards?"

"Yes," Rose said, before her sisters could jump in again. "He asked me to marry him. We were only waiting for your return to make it final. But it turns out he wasn't wealthy after all—or well, he was, but on stolen money."

"What are we going to do?" Aunt Farmington asked piteously. "The girl has been completely humiliated in the eyes of society. Absolutely *everyone* knew of their engagement."

"Not a problem, Aunt Farmington," Lord Pemberton-Howe said cheerfully. He chucked Thalia under her chin, even though she stood nearly as tall as him. "Do not fret, my dear graces. All is not lost."

# 27

"No?" Thalia asked skeptically.

"Where have *you* been, Papa?" Rose asked, eager to change the subject from her own woes.

Lord Pemberton-Howe disentangled himself from his daughters. He moved to sit down in the chair by the empty fireplace as the maid came in to deliver the tea that had been ordered.

"I have been to Pemberton, just as I told you . . . er, I did tell you that that's where I was going, didn't I?"

"You mentioned it briefly before leaving," Rose said, sitting on the sofa and busying herself with pouring out tea for her aunt and father. Somehow, this prosaic action, together with her father's unexpectedly cheerful manner, served to calm her roiling emotions.

"Yes? Well, that's where I was. Turns out that that steward of mine, Mr. Strate, was not so straight after all. He has been fudging the books for the past ten years, and making a tidy profit on it too."

"Oh, no!" the three girls gasped.

"Oh, my lord, what did you do?" Aunt Farmington said, sitting down in the chair opposite his and accepting a cup of tea from Rose.

"I had to go down, naturally, and catch him at it. With the help of my good friend and neighbor, Squire Thompson, we managed to find most of the money Strate had squirreled away."

"But that's wonderful!" Rose cried, handing a second cup to her father.

"No, Rosebud, it is not just wonderful, it is fantastic!" her father said, leaning forward. "It means that we now have enough money to pay all of our bills and more!"

"You mean there is no need for Rose to marry?" Laia asked.

"No! She can do as she pleases. Of course, I would like to see her married someday, but there is no longer the urgency that there was before." He sat back with his tea, and sipped at it as if he hadn't a care in the world.

Rose was astonished. She was dumbfounded. All of her tears and anguish and worry for the past few weeks were for nothing!

"Oh, Rose, isn't it wonderful?" Thalia said, clapping her hands together.

Rose gave a shaky smile. She then took hold of herself and said, "Yes, indeed it is. It is absolutely amazing. I am very happy for you, Papa. Well, for us all."

"Tell us everything, Papa," Thalia said, sitting down at his feet.

He proceeded to tell his long tale—beginning with how he went to Pemberton and surprised his steward relaxing in the manor's main drawing room, drinking fine, expensive brandy.

Rose listened with just half an ear as she thought about the implications her father's discovery had for her.

She didn't need to worry about marrying. She didn't need to worry about Lord Kirtland or Sinjin. She could pay her bills and her debt . . . No. She supposed she no longer owed that debt, since Lord Kirtland had fled the country.

All of her problems were solved!

Then why did she still feel so empty and sad?

She just could not understand it. Perhaps she was just tired from so much emotional upheaval.

Yes, that must be it. She must just be very tired.


Sinjin sipped at his brandy. He hadn't taken the time to enjoy the quiet, unobtrusive company at Whites in a while. But then, he had been rather preoccupied the past few weeks.

He nearly laughed at the understatement, and if things had worked out differently perhaps he would have actually laughed. But not now.

He could not fathom how he was going to live without seeing Rose. He had known before he had told her about Kirtland that he would be risking his friendship with her. But he'd had to tell her. He'd had to try.

It had hurt that she hadn't believed him. And it hurt even more because she had hit upon the one thing that he could not deny—his jealousy.

Despite everything she had done and said, he still loved Rose. She was a vital part of his life. So much so that just the thought of never seeing her again . . . He finished off the rest of the brandy in his glass in one gulp.

His only hope at this point was that tear, that one tear that she had hastily wiped away before telling him that he was never to see her again. Had it meant that there still were some deeper feelings in her heart for him? Was that what it had meant, or was that just wishful thinking on his part?

"Fungy, what are you doing sitting here all alone?" Sin asked, settling into the chair next to his.

Sinjin nearly jumped, so deep was he into his own thoughts.

He looked over at his friend, not a little surprised to see him here, and pushed his thoughts to the back of his mind. Mustering up a smile he said, "Just enjoying a moment's peace."

"Been busy since that whole Kirtland business, I suppose?" he asked.

"Yes. I can't tell you how many times I've been asked to repeat the story of how I figured out that it was Kirtland who was leading the gambling scheme."

Merry and Julian came over and joined them with a footman in tow carrying a tray with another bottle of brandy and glasses for all.

"Must be hard being a hero," Merry said, sitting down and pouring out brandy for all of them.

Sinjin paused for a moment and looked around him at Sin, Merry, and Julian.

This was the way it was supposed to be, he thought to himself. This was right. He was in pain and in need of companionship and perhaps some good sound advice. He was in need of his friends—and here they were, without fail.

What a relief it was! He felt his heart immeasurably lighter than it had been not five minutes ago.

Sinjin smiled for an instant and shook his head. "I'm not a hero. I was doing a job that I was asked to do."

"Speaking of which, I've got a bone to pick with you, Cousin!" Merry said, putting down the bottle before he had finished filling all of the glasses.

Sinjin held up his hands. "I plead innocence."

"How could you have accepted a position to work with Parliament without telling any of us?"

"Well, it wasn't really with Parliament, just with Lord Halsbury."

"Yes, and Halsbury was working on Parliament's behalf."

Sinjin gave a shrug. "It was a secret investigation. I couldn't tell you."

As Merry picked up the brandy bottle once more and finished pouring out the rest of the drinks, Sin commented, "I just can't believe you have let us go on believing you to be nothing more than a society buck—and all this time you've been ferreting out master criminals." His eyes were sparkling sardonically in his saturnine face.

Sinjin felt his old resentments flash to the surface. But he knew that Sin meant well, and so forced himself to speak lightly. "Well, Sin, if you'd remember, I haven't always been so consumed by fashion. There was a time when I was more concerned with my studies than even you were about yours."

Sin and Merry began laughing. "I remember those days!"

"My God, what a bore you were at times, harping on about reading this playwright or that philosopher! At least you did take time out to have some fun with us every so often," Merry said.

"We were practically inseparable!" Sinjin exclaimed.

"Yes, but you were always harping on about your studies," Sin complained.

"I loved the classics," Sinjin agreed.

"Still do, I suppose," Julian said.

"Do you?" Merry asked.

"I've caught him twice over the past few weeks. Once reading Greek, and quoting it to me! And the other day, writing in it," Julian said, helping himself to one of the glasses of brandy.

"I can't believe you've kept that up," Sin said, shaking his head.

"I think there's a lot about me that you've forgotten, or just don't realize," Sinjin said quietly, looking at Merry.

Merry had the grace to look uncomfortable for a moment. "Fungy . . ."

He held up his hand. "It's all right, Merry. I've already beaten you to a bloody pulp about it. Although I must admit, you choosing Sin to be the baby's godfather certainly got me thinking. It hurt me, but it made me take a good hard look at my life."

He took a sip of his brandy. "Well, that and nearly losing my life."

"Nearly losing your life? When did that happen?" Merry asked, sitting forward.

Sinjin told them briefly about saving Miss Thalia Grace from the river and the consequences—how it had been the final straw to his decision to make some major changes in his life.

His friends were all stunned into silence, until Merry finally said, "I can't believe you didn't tell us."

Sinjin shrugged. "You were all so busy with your own lives. We haven't been seeing very much of each other recently."

"It's true," Sin said slowly.

"I can't change the demands that my family are making on me . . ." Merry began.

"No, and you shouldn't. Teresa needs you and you should be there for her, no matter what," Sinjin acknowledged.

"But that doesn't mean that you can't come over and share your problems with me, Sinjin," his cousin said, earnestly. "I'm still here."

Sinjin nodded. "Thank you."

"As am I." "And I," Sin and Julian said together.

"Well, then, perhaps you all can think of a way out a little dilemma I seem to be facing right now," Sinjin said, giving his friends a smile.

"Anything!"

"Of course!"

"You met Miss Grace at my little picnic last week," Sinjin began.

"Became engaged to Kirtland that day, didn't she?" Sin asked.

Sinjin nodded. "That was the whole point of the party. I'd gone to her home to ask her to marry me, and . . . well, she told me that she was hoping for a proposal from Kirtland—before I said anything, luckily."

"You were going to propose to her?" Merry was astonished.

"Finally found someone to make you forget Georgiana," Sin said, nodding his head.

Sinjin gave him a little smile. "With Georgiana's full approval, of course."

"But now that Kirtland is gone, she is free again," Julian pointed out.

"Exactly," Sinjin said. "Only problem is that I tried to warn her about Kirtland before I told Halsbury. Needless to say, she didn't believe me. Accused me of lying, acting out of jealousy and finally told me never to see her again."

"Oh dear," Julian said.

"Makes things a little difficult," Merry agreed.

"Not going to give up, are you?" Sin asked.

Sinjin smiled. "No!"

His friends laughed approvingly at that, and then huddled together.

"We'll come up with something. Have no fear, Fungy," Julian said, giving him a pat on the shoulder.

"That's just what I was counting on."

# 28

Rose was just finishing her sampler when her aunt joined her in the drawing room the following day.

"Have you given a thought to what you will wear this evening?" Aunt Farmington asked.

Rose looked up. "I was not planning on going out this evening."

Not after the countless hours of sleep she had lost the past few nights just thinking about Sinjin.

She could still see his sad face in her mind's eye when she had called him a liar and told him that they should not see each other ever again. It haunted her—her happy, always smiling Sinjin looking so miserable.

"What do you mean? Tonight is Lady Wynworth's rout. You *must* attend," her aunt said, erasing the horrible picture from her mind and bringing her back to the present.

"If I go, I am certain to be the laughingstock of the party," Rose said, stabbing her needle through the material of her sewing.

And if she went, she would surely meet Sinjin.

What would she do if she were to meet him? Would she have to turn away? Would he? No, there was no way around it. The best thing to do would be to simply not go to any more society parties.

The thought of life without Sinjin . . .

Rose squeezed her eyes shut for a moment to stop the stinging of her tears.

"And if you do not go, do you think it will be any better?" her aunt asked.

Rose kept her eyes down on her work. "No, but at least I won't have to hear the horrible things that people are saying about me."

"Rose Grace, do not tell me that you are afraid to face your detractors?"

Rose blinked to clear her eyes, set down her sewing once again, looked straight at her aunt and said, "I am afraid to face my detractors."

*And Sinjin.*

Aunt Farmington laughed. "No, you are not. And if you are, I shall not allow you to be. You *will* attend the rout this evening."

"No . . ." Rose began, but was interrupted by Reynolds, the butler, who walked into the room followed by Lady Huntley and Lady Reath.

Rose stood up, fondly remembering the wives of two of Sinjin's closest friends. She had met them at his picnic—could it have been only a week ago?

"I beg your pardon, ma'am, but Miss Grace has visitors." Reynolds announced the ladies and then left the room.

"What a pleasant surprise! Please come in," Aunt Farmington said to the two ladies.

"Thank you," Lady Huntley said, her bright blue eyes looking openly and sympathetically at Rose. Rose felt herself warm at her obvious sincerity.

"We came by to see how you were, Miss Grace," Lady Reath added, settling her petite frame on the sofa Aunt Farmington had indicated, "and to ask if you were planning on attending Lady Wynworth's party this evening." She was as direct and straightforward as Rose remembered.

Aunt Farmington gave Rose a significant look.

"I was not planning on doing so," Rose said, ignoring her aunt.

"But you must!" Lady Reath said, emphatically.

"Yes, really," Lady Huntley added, in a quieter tone. "If you do not, your position in society will be jeopardized."

"And everyone may think that you knew about Lord Kirtland's dishonest activities," Lady Reath added bluntly.

Rose was taken aback by this. "Do you really think so?" she asked, beginning to be seriously worried, not only for her own reputation, but for that of her sisters and father as well.

"Absolutely," they said together.

"I told you, my dear, you *must* attend this rout," Aunt Farmington said, adding her voice to their argument.

Rose looked from one lady to the next. But if she went . . . how was she to avoid Sinjin? Did she *really* want to avoid him? If she went, she might see him again.

Lady Huntley gave her a warm smile. "Do not worry, Miss Grace. We will be there with you, and between us and our husbands, no one will dare to say anything unkind to you."

The thought of not seeing Sinjin ever again was unbearable. And just thinking about being with him made her heart feel so much lighter and happier. She would decide later what she would say to him—if she was given the opportunity.

Rose returned Lady Huntley's smile gratefully. "Thank you, my lady. You are much too kind."

"Not really. We just care about . . ."

"It is no problem at all," Lady Huntley said, interrupting Lady Reath and giving her a fierce look.

"Now, first of all, you must agree to call us by our given names, and we shall call you by yours, for we are going to be fast friends before you know it."

Rose nodded her head and laughed, feeling better already. Somehow, with the support of these two very kind ladies, she felt as if she could face nearly anything—social opprobrium and Sinjin.

"And secondly," Lady Huntley continued, "you must show us what you are going to wear, because, as I am certain you know, you must look magnificent to face down the *ton*."

And bowl Sinjin over as well, Rose added in her own mind.

Rose could not deny that she was nervous that evening when she entered Lady Wynworth's party. She still had not decided what she would say to Sinjin when they met.

She thought that maybe she would try to apologize, but that seemed to be too little. Of course, throwing herself at his feet would be a bit overdramatic.

She smiled at the thought but with an edge of panic in her mind. She needed some sort of happy medium, but so far she had not hit upon just the right thing.

But there was one thing that Rose could deny no longer—St. John Fotheringay-Phipps had become such an integral part of her life that she could not imagine life without him. And tonight, she had to do everything and anything she could to get him back into it—even if it meant literally throwing herself at his feet.

Rose and her aunt met Cassandra and her husband, Lord Huntley, just inside the door to Lady Wynworth's main drawing room, as they had agreed.

"Excellent, Rose. I knew that green gown would

look stunning on you! And the new gold trim really makes you stand out," Cassandra said, looking Rose over approvingly.

Rose swallowed nervously. "Thank you. I promise to buy you more of this wonderful trimming as soon as . . ."

"Pish-posh! Don't even think about it. I told you this afternoon, I bought it on a whim and didn't even know which dress I might sew it on to. It looks perfect on you—and I am happy to have had something to liven up your rather plain dress. And cutting the neckline down has helped a great deal, just as I told you it would."

Rose could feel her face heat when she thought about how much flesh she was displaying this evening. However, as had been pointed out by Cassandra and Sara, it was no more than every other lady present, and a good deal less than some.

Cassandra turned to her husband, who was looking quite handsome—his black coat setting off his black hair, dark complexion and stunning bright blue-green eyes. Of course, Rose much preferred Sinjin's dark blond locks and laughing blue eyes, but Lord Huntley's looks were definitely striking, especially when next to his fair wife with her lovely blond hair and pale blue eyes.

"Rose is looking quite pretty, isn't she, Julian?" Cassandra said.

Lord Huntley bowed. "I could not agree more, my love. Very pretty, Miss Grace, you are looking very pretty."

Rose felt her face grow warm at his attention, but she curtsied and mumbled her thanks.

Lord Reath and his wife, Sara, joined them just then, so Rose had to endure another round of compliments and exclamations over how good the new trimming looked on her dress. If Rose didn't know that they honestly meant well, she would have thought that they were overdoing it just a little. But after having spent the afternoon with both ladies, she knew that they had only the best intentions for her.

"You clearly have no need of me this evening, Rose. I shall leave you to your friends," her aunt said, before setting off to find one of her numerous friends with whom to spend her evening.

Rose watched her go with a little trepidation. Without her aunt there to support her, she would be completely dependent on her new friends to see her through what she was sure would be a difficult evening. She sincerely hoped her trust was not misplaced.

# 29

The group of friends proceeded further into the overcrowded room and approached the dance floor, where a country dance was just forming.

"Would one of the most beautiful ladies in attendance grant me the honor of this dance?" a gentleman said, coming up just next to Rose.

She turned to see Lord Merrick bowing to her, with a twinkle of mischief in his eyes.

Rose laughed and flushed once again. "La, sir, you could not be referring to me," she said, jumping right into playing his game.

"But who else would I be speaking to?" he asked.

Rose looked to her other side, where Cassandra was standing and watching this lighthearted play. "Why, to Lady Huntley, of course," Rose said, stepping aside so that Cassandra was closer to Lord Merrick.

He shook his head. "She is indeed one of the prettier ladies present, but I believe Julian might be tempted to call me out if I were to tell her so."

Rose and Cassandra laughed, and Lord Huntley, upon hearing his name, turned back to them to see what was going on. But Lord Merrick could not be put off so easily. Once again, he held out his hand to Rose.

"Oh yes, do dance with Merry, Rose. It will do wonders for your reputation. You must be seen dancing with as many gentlemen as possible. That way, the gossips will not have so much fodder to chew on."

Rose could see Cassandra's point—the more she was seen as being accepted, especially by gentlemen in as good a social position as Lord Merrick, the better it would be for her reputation.

Gratefully, she took Lord Merrick's hand and allowed him to lead her onto the dance floor. Cassandra and Lord Huntley followed them.

Rose felt as if the entire room was watching as she and Lord Merrick turned and skipped about in the dance. If it were not for his reassuring smiles and for Cassandra next to her, she was sure she would have succumbed to the temptation to run and hide in the ladies' withdrawing room.

It had not been above two minutes after the dance had ended that Lady Jersey approached Rose, with a little smirk on her face.

"Good evening, Miss Grace. I must say, I am surprised to see you here," she said.

Rose felt herself stiffen. This was exactly what she had been fearing all evening.

"Surely you would not expect her to shut herself away because she had been deceived, along with everybody else?" Sinjin said, strolling up from behind Rose at a leisurely pace.

Rose spun around. *Sinjin!*

Lady Jersey turned to face her opponent. "You always believe the best in everyone, Fungy."

He gave a little bow. "Indeed, I do. Believe that you would not wish to destroy a girl's reputation simply because she misjudged a fellow. As you did yourself, Lady Jersey. You were the one who insisted on granting Kirtland vouchers to Almack's, were you not?"

The lady blushed a dull red. "Well, anyone can make a mistake. Why, we were all taken in by Lord Kirtland."

"Yes, indeed, we were." Sinjin turned to Rose as Lady Jersey moved quickly on.

Rose started to breathe again, not even having fully realized that she had stopped.

Sinjin took her hand gently in his and looked at her with genuine concern. "How *are* you, Rose?"

"Much better now that you are here," she said, quietly, and then realized that she had spoken her thoughts out loud. She stole her hand back from Sinjin and pressed it to her now flaming cheeks.

Sinjin just laughed. "Can't tell you how happy I am to hear that."

"Sinjin . . ." Rose began. But he gave his head a quick shake as if to say, "not here."

The orchestra played the introduction to a waltz, and Sinjin held out his hand and gave her a small bow. "Would you care to dance, Miss Grace?"

"Er, oh, yes. Thank you," Rose answered.

Once again, as they made their way to the dance floor, Rose felt as if every eye was on her. She was sure of it when she looked about her and saw Lady Jersey and Countess Lieven standing by the side, watching her and whispering to each other.

"Do not pay them any mind," Sinjin said firmly.

She looked back at Sinjin. He was smiling and looking like he hadn't a care in the world—just like always.

"Perhaps if you stopped looking like a frightened deer, and instead placed a small smile on your beautiful lips, it might help."

Rose gave a little laugh. "I am sorry."

"No need to apologize. That's better." He nodded approvingly as Rose relaxed a little and tried to look as if she were enjoying herself

It was not easy. She felt as if every muscle in her body was wound tight with tension. What was she going to say to him? She had never worked it out, and now . . .

"Is that a new dress? It is extremely flattering," Sinjin said as he gently turned her around with the movement of the dance.

Rose wanted to hug him. He was so wonderful, talking of nothing at all just to ease her tensions.

"No, actually, it is an old dress, but altered a little and with new trimming added. Sara . . . Lady Reath and Lady Huntley came and helped me with it this afternoon."

Sinjin nodded, a smile tugging up one corner of his mouth. "Well, it is extremely becoming. Your sister Laia should wear such a creation. It would enhance her coloring in a very flattering way."

"I shall have to see to that."

They continued to turn about the room, sharing an easy silence. The voices all around them seemed to fade away. Even Lady Jersey's shrill voice, which was so easy to hear, even from a distance, faded to nothing.

It no longer mattered to Rose what other people were saying about her. The only thing she cared about was Sinjin.

This was the time when she had to say something about what had happened between them. "Sinjin . . ." Rose began, not entirely sure of what she was going to say.

He shook his head. "Do not even think about it, Rose. You could not have known."

*How did he know what she was thinking?*

"But the things I said . . ."

"Were entirely understandable. And some were even true," he said.

Rose looked up at him, wondering what he meant.

"You were absolutely right when you said that I was jealous," he explained without her having to ask. "I was very jealous of Kirtland. He had your affection. It was he who you wanted to marry. Not me. And it was because of that that it took me longer than it should have to figure out that it was in fact Kirtland who was the mastermind behind the gambling scheme."

He paused to allow her to go through the open French doors before him. He had waltzed her over to the other side of the room, and was now leading her outside to the garden.

Rose felt as if her head were spinning, but she walked out into the fragrant garden, filled with beautiful colored lanterns lining the walkways. Sinjin's hand was still on the small of her back as he guided her to one of the more remote corners of the garden.

"Georgiana was the one who told me that she thought Kirtland was more than he seemed. It was her suspicions that made me realize that it wasn't just my jealousy speaking—but that there was, in fact, a reason to be suspicious of him."

"Lady Mirthwood knew it was him?"

"No. She didn't know anything about my investigation. She just knew that there was something about Lord Kirtland that made her feel uncomfortable. She is an excellent judge of character, you know."

"But he made me feel uncomfortable too. I thought . . ." Rose could not finish her sentence. She had thought that that feeling meant that she was in love. But now she was beginning to realize that love did not have to be uncomfortable.

In fact, she thought it could be very comfortable indeed.

"You think a great deal," he said quietly.

Sinjin was standing very close to her now. His overwhelming male presence made Rose not only feel comfortable, but safe and secure. She wanted nothing more than to rest her head on his shoulder and to feel him wrap his arms securely around her.

"Too much," she agreed.

He bent down and very gently pressed his lips to hers.

Immediately, Rose felt a rush of tingles through her body. Warmth followed, welling up in her breast. Without worrying about what he would think of her, or whether or not she was doing the right thing, she allowed herself to just relax and kiss him back.

And she also found that she needed to wrap her arms around his neck and hold on to him—just in order for her knees not to completely give way.

It felt so good, so right to be in Sinjin's arms.

Perhaps this, too, was love? This warm, wonderful feeling of being with a man who didn't put you on edge, but instead took the edge away and made you feel treasured and comforted.

"Rose," Sinjin said, when they finally separated. "I know you were in love with Lord Kirtland, but perhaps . . ."

"But I don't know that I was," Rose interrupted.

"You don't?"

"No. I thought I needed to marry Lord Kirtland—because he was wealthy, and it was the only way for our family to be able to pay our bills. I know how he made me feel, but it was nothing like this, Sinjin. You make me feel . . . cherished . . . loved."

Sinjin laughed a quiet little laugh. "Well, then, my love, say that you will marry me instead. I may not be as wealthy as Kirtland, but at least my money has come to me honestly."

Rose had to laugh. "It's all right, you know. My father

just found that his steward was stealing him blind. So we no longer need to worry about our finances.

"And," she continued, looking deeply into his eyes, "I no longer need to marry a wealthy husband. Now I can marry simply for love."

Sinjin's lips pressed against hers once again. And then, before she knew it, he was deepening his kiss, sending even more tingles down her body. She pressed herself even closer to him as he in turn drew her against him.

A discreet cough and a giggle made them jump apart.

"Er, thought you might be needing a chaperon," Lord Merrick said.

"Or six," Lady Merrick added, still giggling.

Rose felt her color rise as she realized that all of Sinjin's friends and their wives were standing about, discreetly admiring the flowers and the colored lanterns.

"And I seem to remember a certain cousin of mine reprimanding me for hanging on my wife's arm a few years ago," Lord Merrick said, with laughter in his voice.

Sinjin too began to laugh. "Back when I didn't know any better, I assure you, Cousin."

"Well, at least they don't always argue with each other," Lord Reath said, giving his wife a significant look.

"Well, but he doesn't try to manage her life for her at every turn," she said laughing, as she reached out to take her husband's hand affectionately.

"And they are both impeccably dressed," Cassandra said.

"And can quote Greek to each other to their heart's content," Lord Huntley added.

"Yes, I think they make a perfect match," Lord Merrick said.

"Shall we place a wager on it—perhaps over a hand of whist?" Sinjin asked.

"NO!" came the reply, loudly and in unison.

Rose laughed, looking adoringly at her handsome, witty, clever Sinjin, and took his hand firmly in hers. Hand in hand, they joined the three other couples, the sound of merry laughter warmly cocooning them all.

## AUTHOR'S NOTE

How sad an ending is. When you get to the end of a good book (as I hope you found this one to be) you just want it to go on. That is how I felt about this series of books, which I have begun calling The Merry Men Quartet. However, just as every good book must end, so too, must my quartet.

Merry, Sin, Julian, and Fungy will always remain the best of friends and now that they are all married, we know that they will continue to live full and happy lives (at least in our minds).

If you have not yet read the other books in the series, they are: *Miss Seton's Sonata*, Merry, aka Richard Angles, the Marquis of Merrick's story; *Wooing Miss Whately*, the story of Sinclair Stratton, Viscount of Reath; and *Love of My Life* which tells how Julian Ritchie, Earl of Huntley came from Calcutta and joined the friends. This is the order in which the books were published, however the correct chronological order for them is actually *Love of My Life*, then *Wooing Miss Whately*, followed by *Miss Seton's Sonata* and finally, Fungy's (or if you prefer, Sinjin's) book.

Please look for all of these books wherever you normally buy books. More information on them, the Regency period, and my future books can be found at www.meredithbond.com. And finally, I would love to hear from you, so do write to me at P.O. Box 341413, Bethesda, MD 20827.

# More Regency Romance
# From Zebra

# Discover the Romances of
# **Hannah Howell**